The Hand of God

by
John Isaac Jones

Table of Contents

Bobby 5
Argument 13
Sugar Mill 19
Carmelo's 24
Idella 30
Big Job 35
Sheriff Cunningham 39
Lazarus 45
Fight at Carmelo's 54
Little Engine 59
Happy Days 64
Shakedown 69
The Agreement 76
Murders 82
Monster 94
Lost Soul 99
Newspaper Article 103
Seeking Peace 107
Little White Church 113
Singing at the Beach 119
Visit with Lucky 122
Baptism 127
Mother's Love 133
Jail 137
Arraignment 142
Bags Calhoun 148
Answers 155
Christmas Conversation 162
District Attorney 167
New Negotiations 174
Investigation 178
"Big Walter" Huffman 185
Lucky's Trial 193
Bobby's Testimony 199
Cross Examination 205
Surprise Witness 211

Phantom Witness 218
Verdict 222
Freedom 229
Lazarus.. 233
Fire.. 237
An Army .45 and Two Clips.. 242
Settling Up.. 247
Shootout.. 251
Reconciliation... 258
Afterword.. 263

John Isaac Jones

For
My most wonderful friend,
Clayton Vandiver

Bobby

September, 1955

Sand River Road was the only way in and the only way out of the small black community at Palm Harbor, Florida. Just over a mile long, the sand and gravel thoroughfare ran due east from Old Dixie Highway, the main road between Jacksonville and Miami, all the way across the Indian River, and ended at the beach. From the first, local whites had no interest in the property along the road. There were far too many horror stories about hurricanes coming in from the ocean, then carrying whole families and their belongings back out to sea. Thus, the earliest settlers were poor black families, mostly migrant agricultural workers, who either couldn't find or couldn't afford property in the nearby town of Wakoola Springs. Thus, by the late 1940s, more than thirty such families were living along either side of the road and, in 1949, a little white-painted church was built just east of the Indian River so the community would have a place to worship and bury their dead. Over the ensuing years, Ebenezer Baptist Church would become a focal point for the little community.

On this particular Sunday morning, the little white church on Sand River Road was filled with parishioners. It was a beautiful September morning in Palm Harbor. Leaves were falling, squirrels were frolicking, the hot days of August were past, and the cool breezes off the Atlantic Ocean were a more-than-welcome relief to residents of the little coastal town. Inside the church, the congregation, some forty strong, were all dressed up in their Sunday best and listening quietly as Rev. Ronald Jenkins delivered his sermon. Seated among the pews were twenty-four-year-old Bobby Lincoln, his common-law wife Idella, and his mother Hattie. Rev. Jenkins, a medium-built, bespectacled man in his early fifties, was pacing slowly back and forth behind the pulpit with an open Bible in his hand.

"Thou shalt not kill," he said. "That is God's sixth commandment. There is no greater sin than taking the life of another human being. Mankind has laws against killing, but God's wrath is far more powerful and those who break the sixth commandment by killing their fellow man will feel God's wrath in all of its great fury."

He stopped, inhaled, and glanced at the clock.

"Well, dear friends, I see the noon hour is almost here and I would like to finish today's worship by singing 'I'll Fly Away.' Then we will close with the final prayer."

There was a shuffling sound as members of the congregation took hymn books, thumbed through the pages, and, at the minister's prompt, began singing.

"Some bright morning when this life is over, I'll fly away. To that home on God's celestial shore, I'll fly away. I'll fly away, oh glory I'll fly away in the morning. When I die, hallelujah by and by, I'll fly away. I'll fly away, oh glory, I'll fly away in the morning. When I die, hallelujah bye and bye, I'll fly away."

Once the song was finished, the minister turned back to the congregation.

"Now let us pray."

The worshippers bowed their heads.

"Oh Lord, we want to thank you for all the blessings you have bestowed upon us. We know that all goodness comes from your hand and, without you, our lives would be poor and filled with sadness. You are the way, the truth, and the light..."

Bobby, bored to tears, raised his head and peered out the window at a squirrel in the live oak tree outside. The squirrel, holding an acorn in its paws, was furiously nibbling through the hard outer shell to reach the soft meat inside. Since each of the church's rectangular window panes had been painted with a single white cross, Bobby had to crane his neck upward to see the fullness of the animal. This stretching movement alerted his mother and, out of the corner of her eye, seeing her son's head was not bowed, she punched his leg. Bobby, with an irritated look, snapped back to attention and bowed his head again. The minister continued.

"Bless all those who are less fortunate and lay your healing hands on the sick and the afflicted that you might heal them and, as always, give us your love and guiding light so that we may follow in your divine footsteps and dwell in the house of the Lord forever."

He paused.

"All of this we pray in your name. Amen."

***

Ten minutes later, Bobby and his family were saying good-bye to the minister on the church's front steps. Bobby's mother was first.

"Miss Hattie, it warms my heart to see you looking so proud and happy on the Lord's day," the minister said.

"Thank you, Rev. Jenkins," she said. "The Lord has blessed me in so many ways."

The minister smiled.

"You know you have a standing invitation from me to come over for supper one night," she continued.

"I appreciate that," the minister replied. "Let me check my schedule and I'll let you know."

Bobby's mother smiled, then moved away.

The minister turned to Bobby, offering his hand.

"So glad you could come join us today," the minister said.

"Thanks," Bobby said.

The minister peered at him.

"Bobby, how long you been coming to our church now?"

"Long time, reverend," Bobby replied with a smile. "Ever since I can remember."

"Don't you think it's time you gave your soul to the Lord?" the reverend asked.

"How do you mean?" Bobby asked.

"On the third Sunday of this month," the minister said, "we're having a baptizing down at Tomoka Creek. Would you like to join us and have Jesus cleanse your soul?"

Bobby peered curiously at the minister. He felt awkward.

"Oh, Bobby," his mother said, stepping forward. "That would mean so much to me. I would just do anything if you would give your heart to the Lord."

Bobby was still unsure as to how he should answer.

"I'm just not sure if I'm ready yet," he said finally. "Let me think about it."

The minister smiled.

"The Lord don't want to take you until you're ready," the minister said. "You'll know when you're ready. And so will the Lord."

"Just give me a little time," Bobby said. "I'll let you know."

"Thanks, Bobby," the minister said. "I'll be waiting to hear from you."

***

Moments later, Bobby and Idella said good-bye to his mother, who lived directly across the road from the church, then started walking along Sand River Road to their home.

"Bobby, you gonna have to get some food in the house," Idella said as they walked. "I'm almost out of flour, there is no butter; only thing we got to eat is eggs. Thank God for them chickens."

"You got enough for tonight, don't you?" he said. "The store is closed on Sunday. I can't buy anything until tomorrow."

"I can make biscuits and eggs and you can have biscuits and syrup, but there is no butter."

"That will be okay," Bobby said. "When I get off work tomorrow, I'll buy some things."

"I just hope we can get by until then," Idella said.

He glared at her.

"Now don't start," he said. "I'm in no mood to listen to your nagging."

"I don't want to nag," she said. "But there is no food in the house. You've got to do something."

"I know! I know!" Bobby said. "I've heard it a thousand times. I'll get some things when I get off work tomorrow. Just give me a list."

"And I need firewood for the cook stove," she said. "I can't cook without firewood."

"All right! All right, just lay off me. I'll get some firewood soon as I change clothes."

They walked quietly, but Idella wasn't finished.

"When we moved in together, you agreed to do your part! Remember?" she said angrily. "What happened?"

"Come on and shut up!" Bobby said, taking a faster pace and moving ahead.

She stopped, anger in her eyes, arms akimbo.

"What did you say to me?" she asked.

9

Bobby continued walking ahead, his back to her. His silence only triggered more anger.

"Hey," she shouted. "Did you hear me? I'm talking to you."

Bobby continued to ignore her, refusing to stop or turn around. Finally, seeing she was not going to get a response, Idella begrudgingly followed.

Fifteen minutes later, they had reached their home. Bobby and Idella lived in a four-room clapboard structure that stood at the intersection of Sand River Road and Coast Trail, a short stretch of sand and gravel firmament that ran due south along the coast. Less than fifty yards from the beach, the house had been built in 1951 as a weekend getaway by a businessman who lived at nearby Wakoola Springs, but after a 1953 hurricane carried the roof and the owner's dog out to sea, he abandoned the structure. Several days later, when Bobby was returning from fishing, he saw the owner supervising the carpenters and asked about renting it. He and Idella had been living with his mother for several months and he wanted his own place so they could have some privacy. The owner said that once the roof was rebuilt, he would rent it to Bobby for five dollars a month. There were some boards missing on the north side and several stones had fallen out of the chimney, but Bobby had promised to repair those.

***

Twenty minutes later, dressed in overalls, a white, short-sleeved t-shirt, and barefooted, Bobby was at the small shed in the backyard. Inside, he grabbed an axe, checked the blade, then headed toward the beach. As he made his way along the footpath through the thick fan palmetto and mangrove, he knew Idella was right. Lately, they hadn't had enough food in the house. A major reason was that he no longer had an outboard engine for his boat. Bobby had lived on the ocean long enough to know that, if he could get out on the water, he could get all the food he wanted.

For years, he had fished along the coastline and put food on the table for him and his mother, then later for himself and Idella. He was a master fisherman. Now, without an engine, he could paddle out into the ocean at low tide with oars and catch a few fish, but it wasn't like having an engine, which allowed him to zip easily along the coastline and in and out of the coves and inlets quickly to fish the places he had known since he was a youngster. Another reason for the food shortage was money. Although he had been working three days a week at the sugar mill and getting occasional work at the dock, it seemed he never had enough money. Bobby hadn't told Idella, but the previous week, he had lost most of his payday playing *bolitas* at Carmelo's Marina. This meant he couldn't pay the rent. It also meant he couldn't go home with just twelve dollars, so he borrowed twenty dollars from Lucky Holzafel, the charter boat captain who had been his long-time friend and employer at the dock.

Moments later, Bobby arrived at the beach. At high tide points along the beach, the endless waves of salt water had slowly but surely killed the scrub palmetto. All along the edges of the grove, dead palmetto stalks lay brown and rotting in the hot sun. Bobby learned long ago they made excellent firewood, but they had to be cut away and chopped up into small pieces to fit into the family cook stove. Without hesitation, he pulled back the spiny tops and started chopping away. In some thirty minutes, he had cut up a huge pile of stalks, more than enough for a week's supply, then began carrying them in armloads to the house. Back at the house, he used the chop block to cut the stalks into six and eight-inch lengths. Once finished, he carried the stalks to the back porch and stacked them neatly beside the back door so Idella would have easy access to them.

Argument

Late that afternoon, as darkness fell, Bobby and Idella were having their evening meal of scrambled eggs, biscuits, and cane syrup.

"Why are you so quiet?" he asked, taking a bite of eggs.

"I just don't have anything to say," she said.

"If you can't talk to me, who you gonna talk to?"

She shook her head.

"I don't know what we're gonna do," she said.

A long silence. Bobby could see where the conversation was going.

"If you're talking about food and money again," he replied, "I told you I'd take care of that tomorrow."

She didn't reply at first.

"It's not just that," she said finally. "It seems we just live hand to mouth day after day after day."

"You got a roof over your head and food in your mouth," Bobby replied. "It may not be steak and potatoes, but it's enough to fill your stomach."

"I've just never lived like this," she said. "When I was at home, we always had plenty of food in the house."

Bobby could feel his anger rising.

"Complain! Complain! Complain!" he said. "That's all I ever get from you."

"You just let everything go!" she shot back. "The food, the hole in the roof, the chicken coop. I've asked you ten times to fix the door on the chicken coop and it still hasn't been done. You just don't take care of things."

He didn't answer.

"You been playing *bolitas* again?"

"No!" he lied.

"You better not," she said. "If you come in here and tell me you lost yo payday again on *bolitas*, I'm walking out the door."

There was a long silence.

Finally, Bobby spoke. He was calmer now.

"Tuesday, I'll fix the hole in the roof and the chicken coop," he said. "I got to buy some tar before I can fix the roof."

"And you don't have money for that either?" she asked. "Am I right?"

Bobby didn't want to listen anymore. He cleaned his plate, got up from the table, and went to sit on the couch.

"No, don't think you can get away by just getting up from the table," Idella said.

"I'm not thinking anything," he said. "I've finished eating."

A long silence.

"Look!" he said. "I'll do better. Right now, I don't have an engine for the boat. When I get an engine, I'll put all the fish on that table you can eat."

"I hope we can get by until then," she said.

Now, at the second mention of the food question, his anger was rising.

"Why do you keep harping on that?" he asked. "I'm telling you, you ain't going hungry."

"And I'm telling you, all I got for your lunch tomorrow is boiled eggs and cold biscuits."

"I'm fine with that," he said. "I never had cakes and pies on my table when I was growing up."

"Well, I DID," she said. "When I was growing up, my daddy always made sure there was plenty of food in the house."

He shook his head in disgust.

"Yeah, I've heard that story a hundred times," he said. "Your daddy was the greatest man that ever lived. He put lots and lots of food on the table. He had plenty of meat and vegetables and cakes and pies. Yo daddy had food running out of his ears."

"Don't you talk like that about my daddy!" she shouted. "You hear me?"

Instantly, she got up from the table and strode across the room to face him where he was seated on the couch.

"I'm just waiting to hear it again!" he said. "'Oh, my daddy this and oh, my daddy that. He had more food than...'"

Suddenly, livid with anger, she stepped forward, bent over, and slapped him. The sound of the slap reverberated across the room.

For a long moment, Bobby glared at her in anger. Then, suddenly, he sprang up from the couch, took her by the shoulders, and shook her.

"Don't ever hit me!" he shouted, shaking her violently. "Do you understand? Don't you ever hit me!"

Then he pushed her roughly on the couch. For a moment, angry and hurt, she stared at him, then, crying hysterically, she ran into the bedroom and slammed the door.

***

Thirty minutes later, all was quiet. Bobby peeked into the bedroom. Idella was asleep. Now he could relax and be alone with his thoughts. Quietly, he grabbed an empty fruit jar out of the cupboard, then slipped out the back door. Outside, at the corner of the house, he filled the fruit jar half full of fresh

15

water from a rain barrel, then went into the tool shed. There, under an old tarpaulin, he always kept a bottle of moonshine. For several moments, in the darkness, he fumbled under the tarpaulin until he found the bottle, then went back outside and seated himself on the chop block. Carefully, he opened the bottle and finished filling the fruit jar with the moonshine. He took a long swig and grimaced at the rancid taste. His body shivered as he swallowed.

In the distance, he could see the Atlantic Ocean stretching eastward to the horizon. The sea was calm tonight and, several miles away in the darkness, he could see the ghostly lights of a freighter slowly grinding its way southward to Miami. A low-hanging full moon thrust a silvery path across the water toward him. As the moonshine slowly coursed through his veins, his mind drifted back to the preacher's invitation to be baptized.

Bobby had never been much of a religious man. Although he had gone to church with his mother since he was a small child, Biblical teachings had little or no meaning to him. For him, the miracles, the parables, the various stories designed to teach the glory and wrath of God were little more than fairy tales. He felt religion was for the weak and the old and those whose death was imminent. For him, God and religion was little more than a medicine for those who needed to salve their worries about the afterlife. Of course, he could never tell his mother these thoughts. She would be broken-hearted.

Bobby took another swig. His thoughts wandered back to Idella and their courtship. One afternoon, Bobby was walking from the marina back to his mother's house when he saw Idella standing in front of the dry cleaners on Coast Trail, waiting for her ride. From the very first moment, he was interested. She was thin, petite, had a pretty face, and a light mocha, almost bronze, color. Also, there was a quick, quiet smile and a confident air that inspired respect. That first day, he gave her an inviting smile, but she looked away. Over the next few days, Bobby made it a point to reappear in front of the cleaners at the same hour. Two days later, he saw her again and, this time, she responded with a smile. They started talking. She had graduated high school, was from Manatee, a small town some forty miles south, and was living with an aunt in Palm Harbor while she worked at the cleaners.

Moments before her ride arrived, Bobby invited her to go to the movies with him, but she declined. Two days later, at the same hour, Bobby waited for her again. For the second time, he invited her to the movies and, this time, she accepted. The following Friday night, they took the bus to the Capital Theater in Wakoola Springs where they sat in the balcony, the theater's colored section, and watched the movie. Afterward, they went to Wakoola's colored section, had ice cream, and spent almost two hours talking in the park. Over the next three weeks, they made two more trips to the movies in Wakoola, had four picnics at the beach, and dinner with Bobby's mother. By then, they were a couple. She left her job and moved in with him at his mother's house. Their fight tonight was not the first nor would it be the last. They had frequent fights, but each always recovered quickly.

Bobby took another swig. Tomorrow was Monday and he would go back to work at the sugar mill. In many ways, Bobby felt it was a good job. It paid seventy-five cents an hour and he felt he was treated fairly.

Lately, Bobby had only been getting three days a week, but he expected to get more as October and the full harvest season drew nearer. He needed to ask around about a new engine. Also, he had to pay Lucky the fifty-eight dollars he owed him. Part of it he could work off, but he would have to come up with some cash somehow. Now, as he peered across the ocean, he could feel the moonshine dulling his senses. He could feel the laziness in his movements and started to feel sleepy. Finally, he tossed off the last swig of shine, went into the house, and crawled into bed.

Sugar Mill

The following morning, promptly at sunrise, Bobby was out of bed. Once shaved and washed, he put on fresh overalls and a short-sleeved T-shirt, grabbed his lunch pail, and headed out the door. Idella was still asleep. Outside, Bobby crossed the yard and started to walk the mile down Sand River Road to the sugar mill.

Although it was not quite 8 a.m., the Florida sun was a glowering mound of yellow peeping over the eastern horizon. As Bobby walked, his gait and stride spoke of a certain unmistakable confidence. At just over six feet, he had a lean face and a strong jaw. He looked like the kind of man who, when he wanted something, was not afraid to go all out to get it. High overhead, a flock of pelicans flying in a broken-V formation glided quietly.

Ahead, Bobby could see Train, another sugar mill worker, standing in front of the boarding house where he lived. He was waiting to walk to work with Bobby. Train, a tall Jamaican man with a thin face and a flat nose, was in his early thirties. He wore dreadlocks and a New York Yankees cap. Other than the fact that he was in the States illegally, little was known about him. His real name was Night Train Vereen, but everybody just called him "Train."

"Morning, Bobby," he said.

"Morning, Train," Bobby replied. "How you doing today?"

"Not too good," Train replied. "The Tigers beat the Yankees last night. I lost six dollars on a parlay."

"You know anybody that's got a little outboard for sale?"

"You talked to Lucky?" Train said. "I heard him say last weekend he knew a guy trying to sell one."

Bobby perked up.

"Really?" he said. "Did he say who it was?"

"Naw," Train replied. "You'll have to ask him."

Bobby peered at him.

"I'll do that," Bobby said.

They walked quietly.

Train peered up at the electric line above them, then turned to Bobby.

"Bobby," he said, pointing. "See those two birds sitting up there?"

Bobby peered up at the birds.

"Yeah!"

"Bet you a dollar the one on the left flies first."

Bobby laughed.

"Naw, I'm not interested," he said with a laugh. "You don't ever get too far away from gambling, do you?"

"It's the only thing that makes life interesting," Train said. "I've got something to hope for when I'm gambling."

Bobby didn't reply. They walked quietly.

Some ten minutes later, they saw Clifford Parker, another sugar mill worker, standing at the road, waiting to join them. Clifford, a stocky, bespectacled, forever-smiling man in his early fifties, had a jowly face, a slight paunch, and always wore a baseball cap. Clifford lived next door to Bobby's mother and the two had known one another for over twenty years. As they approached, Clifford was reading a newspaper.

"Cliff," Bobby said. "You know where I can buy a little outboard engine?"

"No," Clifford replied, folding the paper and stuffing it under this arm. "But I got some guns for sale. Need a .38 special? An army .45?"

"What would I do with a gun?" Bobby replied. "I'm not in the army anymore."

"Sorry," Clifford said. "I can't help you with the engine."

Ten minutes later, the trio were walking across the wooden bridge that spanned the Indian River. From this vantage point, Bobby could see the lay of the land in all directions. To the south, a lone boatman fished quietly on the west side of the river. To the east, a hungry osprey dipped into the water, grasped a fish, then lifted off into the nearby grove of cypress and mangrove to enjoy its meal. Looking north, Bobby could see Coronado Inlet, the old lighthouse, and the huge rocks that made up the tide break for the inlet. To the west, more than a mile away, he could see the upper stories of the Wakoola County Courthouse and the businesses along Dixie Highway.

Moments later, the trio was across the Indian River and, some fifty yards ahead, the sugar mill came into view. Some five miles inland, in the deep glades, the Devereaux Sugar Company owned more than five hundred acres of rich farmland where the sugar cane was grown. Once harvested, trucks delivered the stalks to the mill for processing. As the three approached the mill grounds, they could see several huge piles of cane stalks waiting to be processed.

"Look at all that cane," Clifford said. "Bet we'll be here until sundown."

"Fine with me," Train said. "I need the money. I owe Carmelo sixty dollars for *bolitas*."

Clifford looked at him.

"That's dangerous," he said. "Real dangerous."

"Why you say that?" Train asked.

"You might be getting a visit from his boys…"

"This ain't the first time I owed him," Train said. "He knows I always pay."

Clifford looked at him.

"Good luck," he said.

***

Bobby spent the day running the mill's extractor, squeezing gallons upon gallons of sweet juice from the sugar cane stalks. Hour after hour, Train and the other workers would trim the leaves off the stalks, then load them into the giant crushing machine where Bobby would reduce them to piles of splintered mush. The work was not physically tiring, but it required constant attention. Bobby had to make sure each load was finished before a new one was begun. Long ago, he had witnessed the nightmare of overloading the machine when a workman had dumped the equivalent of two loads into the hopper. The entire operation had ground to a halt; the overloaded, unprocessed stalks had to be physically removed from the rollers one at a time and the repair process required several hours of down time.

Once the sweet juice was collected, it was moved to a huge, gas-fired vat where it was boiled into a thick liquid. Clifford's job was to bring the vat to a boil, wait until the liquid was at just the right consistency, then turn off the heat and wait for it to cool. Once the thick liquid was cooled to the correct temperature, it was sent to the centrifuges where the rapidly spinning tubes would separate the molasses from the sugar crystals. Clifford, in his role as the mill's "cooler," had the most important job there. He had studied math and engineering at the Negro College in Daytona Beach and was the most educated person at the mill.

At 6 p.m. that afternoon, the shutdown whistle blew and the men, except for Clifford, who agreed to stay late to process the last batch, stopped working. Then each employee lined up to make their mark on the supervisor's sign-out sheet, which gave them credit for the day's work. Carl, the foreman – an early fifties, unsmiling white man who always wore a sweat-stained straw hat – watched as each of the men made their mark on the sheet. Ten minutes later, Bobby and Train were walking back down Sand River Road toward Palm Harbor and Carmelo's Marina.

Carmelo's

In the late forties, after the war, Carmelo's Marina was born in a small cove along the coast at Palm Harbor when Carmelo Sanchez, a Cuban man from Miami, bought five acres of wild palm, mangrove, and pine sapling jungle, cleared it off, and built a small boat dock at the very end of Coast Trail. At the time, there were fewer than one thousand residents in Palm Harbor, but the town was growing and, as it grew, so did the marina. First, there were weekend fishermen and sailing enthusiasts who needed storage and repair services. Next came the shrimpers, the commercial fishermen, and the charter boats. By the early fifties, Carmelo's was a favorite docking spot for the seagoing public and, with the increased traffic, a restaurant and pool hall had been added. Over the years, patrons learned that, in the basement of the pool hall, they could buy moonshine or play *bolitas*, a lottery-style gambling game in which small plastic balls were drawn from a bag. The county had always been dry.

When Bobby and Train entered the restaurant, Bobby saw his friend Lucky Holzafel and Carmelo, the marina owner, sitting at a corner table.

"Bobby!" Lucky called.

Bobby acknowledged the call, then turned to Train.

"I'm going to talk to Lucky," he said.

"I'm going to play *bolitas*," Train said.

Bobby approached Lucky's table.

"Have a seat," Lucky said.

Bobby took a seat.

"Want anything?" Lucky asked.

"No, I can't stay long," Bobby said. "I got to get home. Train said you knew a guy trying to sell a little outboard."

"That's Pee-Wee," Lucky said. "I think he's here now in the pool hall."

"Can you show him to me?"

"Sure," Lucky said. "Come on!"

Lucky stood up and together they started walking across the restaurant floor to the pool hall. Lucky was a strong, physically powerful man. Over six feet, tall and muscular, the native Brazilian was in his late forties, well tanned, and always wore a charter captain's cap. The son of a numbers maker, Lucky came to Palm Harbor from Kansas in the late forties. In Topeka, he had held various odd jobs, including mechanic, fingerprint technician, sheet metal worker, and cab driver. The big Brazilian had fought with Patton's fifth army at the Battle of the Bulge and was decorated with a purple heart. Lucky had a wife in Titusville, or so he said, but Bobby had never met her. Every few months, Lucky would disappear for a few days, then reappear. When Bobby asked where he had been, he would say he had been visiting his wife. His real name was Floyd, but everybody just called him "Lucky."

Moments later, in the pool hall, the smell of smoke, rotgut whiskey, and bathroom freshener hung in the air. Lucky's eyes scanned the players and the pool tables, then he pointed out a small, dumpy man with thick glasses seated on a bench. He was wearing a business suit and watching two others shoot pool.

"That's Pee-Wee," Lucky said.

Bobby peered across the room at the man.

"I should warn you that he doesn't like Negroes," Lucky said. "Just yes sir and no sir and you'll be fine."

"And the two guys shooting pool?" Bobby asked.

"The tall one is Jaybird," Lucky said. "The other one is Dooley."

Bobby peered curiously at the two men shooting pool. He had never seen them before. Jaybird was a slender Cuban man, every inch of six foot four. He had small eyes, a pointy nose, a pencil mustache, and a long forehead. Wearing a black shirt and black tie under a medium purple jacket, he looked like a thug from a Mexican movie. Dooley was a head shorter than his cohort. Decked out in knee-length blue shorts and sandals, he wore a white pleated Cuban shirt, sunglasses, and a stylish, straw-colored Cuban hat with a flowery headband. He looked like a tourist who had just arrived in Miami. Both seemed starkly out of place among the poorly dressed agricultural workers, fishermen, and day laborers.

"I'm going back to the restaurant," Lucky said. "Check with me before you leave? Okay?"

"Sure," Bobby said.

Bobby approached Pee-Wee. Many years earlier, he had learned how to live as a Negro in a white man's world. As a youngster, he remembered seeing his father do the "laugh when it ain't funny and scratch when it don't itch" routine in the presence of white men. Also, he was very familiar with the Negro custom of looking away or at the ground when Negroes spoke to white men. Bobby preferred the second. Scratching and laughing was too much work.

"Good afternoon, sir," Bobby said, not looking in the little man's face. "Are you the gentleman known as Pee-Wee?"

The little man pushed his glasses up on his nose and slowly turned to Bobby.

"That's what they call me."

"Mr. Lucky says you got a little outboard for sale."

"Yeah, I got one."

"What kind?"

"Miller-Scout," the little man said. "Twelve horse. Got the big gas tank."

"That's what I'm looking for," Bobby said. "Can I see it?"

For a moment, Pee-Wee studied Bobby through his thick glasses. Finally, he turned to the two cartoon characters who were shooting pool.

"Hey, boys," he said. "I'm going out here to show an engine to this nigger. I'll be right back."

The tall one nodded his approval.

As they started out, Bobby bristled at the sound of the word "nigger." Normally, any man who called him that – especially another Negro – would have had a fight on his hands, but Bobby stayed calm. He knew how to act around white folks without causing trouble. And he needed an engine.

When Pee-Wee stood up, he was dumpy and ridiculously short, less than five feet tall, had thinning hair, and wore thick Coke bottle glasses.

Despite the short stature, there was no shortage of confidence. As he walked, he had the swagger of a man who was well over six feet. He swung his arms robustly and he carried himself in such a way that he made sure the butt end of the shoulder-holstered pistol inside his coat showed through for all to see.

Outside, Pee-Wee led Bobby across the parking lot to a shiny, new black Cadillac and opened the trunk. Bobby was beside himself with excitement when he saw the engine. It was exactly what he was looking for. It had the big tank that would give him two hours of running time before it needed a refill.

"How much you want?" Bobby asked.

"Forty dollars," Pee-Wee replied.

"Don't you think forty dollars is a little high?" Bobby asked.

"I'm not running a charity," Pee-Wee said. "I should tell you that it's hot. It was stolen off a boat on the St. John's River three months ago."

"I don't care about that," Bobby said. "I need an engine."

"All right," Pee-Wee said. "I'll let you have it for thirty, but that's my best price."

Bobby was lusting after the little engine.

"Well, sir," Bobby said finally, "I'll buy it if you can wait until payday."

Pee-Wee laughed.

"You niggers never have any money," he said. "When's payday?"

"Next Friday."

"I can't make no promises," Pee-Wee said. "If somebody else comes along with the money, I'm going to sell it."

"Yes, sir! I understand," Bobby said. "I promise you I'll be here next Friday night with the money."

"I'll be here," Pee-Wee said, slamming the car trunk shut.

"Thank you for your time, sir," Bobby said.

***

Back inside the restaurant, Bobby found Lucky seated at the same table with Carmelo.

"You going to need me on the *Lady* this week?" he asked.

Lucky's boat was called *Lucky's Lady*.

"Yeah," Lucky said. "Tomorrow. This guy in Wakoola wants to do a four-hour charter. You working at the sugar mill tomorrow?"

"No," Bobby replied. "I'm off."

"Then count on working."

Bobby nodded. "Can you spot me five dollars for a few days?"

"You owe me fifty-eight dollars already," Lucky said.

"Yeah, I know," Bobby said. "I've got into a tight spot lately. I'll work it out with you. You know you always get your money from me."

Lucky inhaled, pulled out a wad of bills, and peeled off a five-dollar bill.

"That's sixty-three dollars you owe me," Lucky said. "Don't spend it all in one place."

Bobby smiled, taking the bill.

"I won't," he said. "Thanks. I'll be at the dock bright and early tomorrow."

Idella

Ten minutes later, Bobby was walking along Coast Trail to Waddell's Grocery. Upon arrival, he bought butter, cheese, coffee, milk, a side of ham, and a small can of tar to fix the roof. Twenty minutes later, as he strode back along the coast road to his home, lugging three bulging sacks of groceries, Bobby assessed his relationship with Lucky. The big Brazilian had been his savior more than once. Before he joined the army, Bobby had worked for Lucky when he was a shrimper. Many days, Bobby worked as a deckhand on Lucky's boat hauling in the nets and delivering the massive tons of shrimp to the fish market at Flagler's Point. During the four years Bobby was in the army, Lucky bought a cabin cruiser he named *Lucky's Lady* and opened a successful charter business. When Bobby returned from military service in Korea, he went straight to Lucky and the big Brazilian put him back to work. If Lucky was getting business, Bobby knew he would have work. Lucky had been good to him in lots of ways. Bobby trusted Lucky.

As he approached his home, he could see smoke coming from the backyard. Idella was boiling clothes in the old wood-fired wash pot. When he rounded the curve in sight of the house, she glanced up and, seeing he was loaded down, ran to help him.

"My! My!" she said with a big smile. "Look at all this!"

"I got you a side of ham," he said.

She peered into one of the bags, smelled its contents, and smiled.

"We gonna eat good tonight!" she said.

After she relieved him of one of the bags, they went into the house together and put away the food. Outside again, Idella doused the fire around the wash pot and, with Bobby's help, fished the steaming clothes out of the pot with an iron rod and into a clothesbasket. While Bobby held the basket, she hung the clothes one by one on the clothesline in the backyard.

***

They had a good meal that night. Idella prepared roast ham, green beans, mashed potatoes with gravy, and biscuits. For dessert, each had a slice of lemon pie. When he was finished, Bobby pushed his chair away from the table as Idella cleaned the table and began washing dishes.

As she stood at the sink, Bobby slipped up behind her and lovingly put his hands around her waist and spun her around to face him.

"That sure was a good meal," he said, peering into her eyes. "Is there going to be any more dessert?"

She laughed.

"You know I've got to have you tonight," she said. "I've been thinking about you all day. It's been three days, so you better be ready."

He smiled.

"I'm always ready for you," he said.

She smiled and kissed him.

"Let me finish these dishes and I'll meet you on the couch."

Some fifteen minutes later, they were snuggled together on the couch, kissing and fondling one another. One by one, articles of their clothing started to fall away and, finally, as the passion intensified, Bobby, completely naked, stood up, picked her up, and carried her to the bed.

Moments later, as he thrust his body into hers, he remembered how much he loved to be with her. As a lover, she was alive and responsive and unafraid. For his every move, she had an equal, efficient countermove. They were not only a good fit, but each knew how to instinctively respond to the other's each and every move. He loved that in her. They were natural lovers. No other way to put it. He had been with other women – several Korean women during his army days, once with a white prostitute in Columbus Georgia, and several other black women – but, as a lover, there had never been another Idella. Afterward, breathing heavily and smelling of raw sex, they rested in one another's arms.

"I love you," Idella said finally.

Bobby didn't respond.

"I love you!" she said again.

Again, he didn't reply.

"Let's go to sleep," he said. "I've got to get up early to go to work."

"No!" she said. "Talk to me! Why can't you tell me you love me?"

He froze at her demands. It was not the first time.

"Answer me," she said. "Why can't you tell me you love me? You tell your mother you love her."

"Yeah," he said. "But that's different. She's my mother."

She studied him for a moment, then she spoke.

"I'm in this relationship because I want it to go somewhere," she said. "If we go on, I want us to be married and have children and a life together. That's the respectable way. Don't you want all that?"

"I enjoy you and, outside the nagging, we get along pretty well," he said. "I just don't think I can commit to something too permanent. At least not now."

32

She withdrew from him.

"Sometimes I think I know you, Bobby," she said. "Other times, I'm not so sure I know you at all."

Bobby sat up and swung his feet over the side of the bed.

"Now don't be running off," she said. "I want you to give me an answer."

Sullenly, he stood up and went to the living room. There, he quickly put on his clothes and started out. As he walked across the kitchen floor, she called to him.

"Bobby!" she shouted. "Come back here and talk to me!"

Moments later, he was outside in the shed, then sitting on the chop block taking a swig of shine. His thoughts drifted back to Idella's question. The answer lay with Olivia Jackson. Bobby had met Olivia in eighth grade math class at George Washington Carver High School. The daughter of a mechanic, she was tall with a slim waist, nice hips, and a pretty face of a medium-dark color, which Bobby admired. They became fast friends at school, but after his father died and he left school, they drifted apart. Then, during the summer he turned eighteen, they met again at a party and started dating. They met for soda pop at Waddell's Grocery, went to Wakoola for movies and ice cream, and took late-night swims in the ocean. Throughout that summer, Bobby was a frequent guest at her parents' house. For the very first time, Bobby was in love. He wrote her love letters, bought her presents, and gave his heart to her lock, stock, and barrel. Then one Sunday afternoon in late August, she announced she had met Odell Wilson and she was going to break up with Bobby. Bobby knew Odell. Odell was a football star at the high school, his father was a dentist in Wakoola, and he had a car. Olivia said she wanted a man with a future. When they parted, Bobby was devastated.

That night, while he and his friend Calvin were talking, he knew he wanted to get as far away from Olivia and Palm Harbor as he possibly could. When Calvin mentioned he had joined the army the previous week, Bobby saw a way out. The next day, Calvin took Bobby to the recruiter in Wakoola Springs and Bobby signed up. When he told his mother, she was heart-broken, but Bobby explained he wanted to get away from Palm Harbor and "see the world while he was young." Also, he said he could get his high school diploma in the service. Three weeks later, Bobby and Calvin were on a bus going to Fort Benning, Ga. for basic training. On the bus, Bobby made a vow to himself. He swore he would never give his heart to another woman like he had to Olivia. The pain and suffering was too great. He cared for Idella and wanted to make her happy, but he vowed he would never do that to himself – or his heart – again. Further, he couldn't tell Idella he loved her unless he truly felt it in his heart. Bobby had to be true to himself. At all costs, he had to do that.

Big Job

The following morning, which was Tuesday, Bobby was at the marina bright and early as promised. Upon arrival, he went straight to *Lucky's Lady* where he found Lucky unpacking two pounds of squid he had bought for bait.

"Morning, Bobby," he said. "There will be four guys on the trip. Rig up two extra rods and reels in case we need them. Check the engine oil and the anchor chain. Also, cut the squid into small pieces. We're going for kings."

Instantly, Bobby set about cutting up the squid. Once that was finished, he raised the engine cover and checked the oil. It needed a quart. Moments later, Bobby was inside the cabin retrieving a quart of oil from underneath Lucky's bunk. Lucky's personal articles were scattered here and there. Bobby had worked with Lucky long enough to know every inch of the *Lady*. Once fresh oil was in the engine and the anchor chain was checked, Bobby started swabbing the deck so it would be clean when the customers arrived. "A good ship is a clean ship," Lucky always said. By 7:45, the boat was ready.

Promptly at eight, the fishing party arrived. The one paying for the trip, a red-faced, middle-aged man named Williard, was talkative and outgoing. They had brought food and beer, hats, and suntan lotion. On charter trips, Lucky liked for Bobby to operate the boat while he socialized with the customers. Once everyone was situated, Bobby fired up the engine and, using the boat's navigation device, headed out to "the big hole," a particularly deep area some six miles offshore where they always caught fish. Once the boat was anchored, they began fishing. The men fished, drank beer, joked, talked about sports and women, and enjoyed themselves. Lucky helped the party members land fish, re-rig and rebait lines while Bobby operated the boat. By 12:30, they had caught more than fifty pounds of fish – kings, cobia, snapper, bonita, and some grouper – and Lucky ordered Bobby to take the boat back in.

Back at Carmelo's, Lucky and Bobby unloaded the fish, helped party members gather personal belongings, and said their good-byes. Once the charter party was gone, they returned to the boat. While Bobby swabbed the deck, Lucky put away the tackle and other gear. It had been a successful charter. Bobby and Lucky made a good team.

"We're finished," Bobby said. "That pays off the five dollars I got from you on Monday."

"That's right," Lucky said. "You still owe me fifty-eight dollars."

Bobby started to leave the boat.

"Before you go," Lucky said. "I want to talk to you about a couple things."

"What you got?" Bobby said, taking a seat on a deck chair.

"I got a big job coming up," Lucky said. "And I want you to help me with it."

"A charter trip?"

Lucky laughed.

"Naw, more than that. Lots more than that."

"What is it?"

"I need for somebody to take the skiff up to Flagler Point one night. All you got to do is bring the boat up the coast to the back of a house. You wait while I go inside. Once I get back, I want you to take the boat out to the Gulf Stream."

"How much does it pay?"

Lucky laughed. "Twenty-five hundred dollars," he said.

Bobby peered at him, then drew back disbelievingly.

"Twenty-five hundred dollars?" he said. "What you going to do? Rob somebody?"

Lucky didn't answer.

"What you going to be doing while I'm running the skiff?"

Lucky looked at him and laughed.

"Are you interested?"

"I don't even know what the job is," Bobby said.

Lucky inhaled, then studied Bobby for a long moment.

"Naw, forget it," he said finally. "I don't think you got what it takes for a job like that."

"How do you know what I got?" Bobby said. "I ain't afraid of nothing."

"Forget it," Lucky said. "Like I said, I don't think you could handle it."

Bobby didn't like to be underestimated.

"Don't say that to me, Lucky," he said. "You know I'm not afraid of anything on this earth."

"Yeah, but you're not ready for this one," Lucky said. "This is big time. You do fine with the small time stuff, but when it comes to the big stuff, you ain't got what it takes. I'll find somebody else."

"You're always ramblin' on," Bobby said. "What's the second thing you wanted to talk about?"

"When are you going to pay me the money you owe me? I really need that money."

"I'll pay you what I owe you," Bobby said. "I always do, don't I?"

"Yeah, I know," Lucky said, "but I need that money now. I've got to have the engine overhauled in the *Lady*. I've got dock fees to pay. I really need that money."

"You're going to have to give me some time," Bobby said.

Lucky fell silent.

"Okay," he said. "I will give you some time. Can you work on Saturday? I got another charter."

"I'll be here," Bobby said.

Sheriff Cunningham

The following day, a Wednesday, Bobby was up at the crack of dawn walking down Sand River Road to his work at the sugar mill. As he walked, he noticed a sheriff's car sitting in front of the boarding house where Train lived. As he approached the boarding house, he didn't see Train waiting as usual. Suddenly, the engine in the sheriff's car started and it headed toward him.

"Bobby!" a voice called.

"Sheriff Cunningham!" Bobby replied, immediately recognizing the man behind the wheel.

"I wanted to tell you that the storm the other night blew a tree down on your daddy's grave," the sheriff said. "Need to go down up there and get it removed."

"Did it knock over the headstone?"

"I'm not sure," the sheriff replied.

"I'll take care of it on Thursday."

"Good enough," the sheriff said. "You doing all right?"

"I'm doing fine," Bobby replied.

"Want me to go down and help you move that tree?"

"No, I'll take care of it," Bobby said.

"Okay!" the sheriff replied. "Don't work too hard today. See you later!"

With that, the sheriff waved good-bye and the county sheriff's car moved on down the road.

Bobby continued walking. Ahead, he could see Clifford patiently waiting in front of his house.

"Not sure why Train didn't meet us today," Bobby said.

"I can tell you why," Clifford said. "He saw Sheriff Cunningham's car out front and he was afraid to come out."

Bobby looked at him with a puzzled look.

"What you mean?"

"Train got into trouble with the law down south," Clifford said. "The last thing he wants to see is a law enforcement officer."

"I didn't know that," Bobby said.

"Ask Train about it," Clifford said. "He'll talk about it."

***

Twenty minutes later, Bobby and Clifford arrived at the sugar mill. Promptly at eight a.m., Bobby fired up the engine for the rollers and started work. Train appeared at work around 9:30 a.m. with the excuse he had overslept. The foreman accepted that and told him he couldn't be late again. An hour later, the crushing machine started to make strange noises. When it got worse, Carl, the foreman, ordered Bobby to shut down the machine so he could inspect it. Once the housing had been removed, Bobby and the foreman could see that the bearings on one of the main rollers had been destroyed.

"We're going to knock off for the rest of the day," Carl said. "I've got to call the repairman."

Moments later, the shutdown whistle blew, the operation was shut down, and Bobby and Train were walking down Sand River Road.

"Clifford was telling me you got into trouble with the law down south," Bobby said.

"Yeah," Train said. "I got involved with some bad people. Spent a little time in jail but got off for lack of evidence."

"What happened?"

"If I tell you, can you keep it under your hat?" Train asked.

"You know I will," Bobby replied.

Train cleared his throat, then began speaking.

"When me and my mama and sister arrived in Fort Pierce from Jamaica, we went straight to Okeechobee and started picking beans. I couldn't believe how much money I was making. I was making eight dollars a day and the three of us could eat for a week on that. Times were good till October, then, when the season was over, the work stopped. I went about a month without working and my mother and sister didn't have food. We was living off the fruit we could steal from trees at night..."

Train hesitated.

"So what did you do?" Bobby asked.

"Well, I had been hanging at the pool hall looking for some kind of work when these two men asked me if I wanted to make two hundred dollars. I asked what they wanted me to do and they said it was a disposal job. What kind of disposal? I asked, and they said they were going to move some things from an old barn out into the Glades. I asked what they were going to move, but they wouldn't tell me. Well, I was desperate, so I didn't ask any more questions and told them I was their man. That night, I went with these two men to an old barn in Okeechobee and we loaded up four bodies and took them deep into the swamps and dumped them in a canal. One of the men said the alligators would eat them. When they paid me, they said if I ever mentioned it, I would be a dead man."

Train stopped.

"That was it?" Bobby asked.

"Well, sort of," Train continued. "About two months later, the police came and arrested me and asked me all these questions and I denied everything. Finally, the police let me go, but I knew if I said anything, I would be gone from this earth."

The two walked quietly.

"Aren't you afraid they'll come after you?" Bobby asked.

"They won't do anything until they think I've crossed them," Train said. "What's more, they would kill my mother first."

"What?" Bobby said.

"That's the way they work," Train said. "If they want you to stay quiet, they let you know your mother will pay first. They told me they knew where my mother lived in Fort Pierce."

"Aren't you afraid for your mother?"

"Not as long as I keep my mouth shut," Train replied.

"Damn!" Bobby said. "That's downright vicious right there."

"That's the way they work," Train said. "They know a man loves his mother more than anybody else on earth, so they use it to control you."

During the conversation, they had walked across the Indian River and were now in sight of the church and Bobby's mother's house.

"I'm going to stop and visit my mother," Bobby said. "I'll see you later."

Moments later, Bobby stepped off Sand River Road and was walking across his mother's yard. The moment he mounted the front porch steps, he knew his mother had been baking fried apple pies.

"Mama!" he called.

"Come on in!" she said. "I'm in the kitchen."

When his mother greeted him, she knew immediately what he wanted and dished four small pies off the stove and placed them on the table.

"Sit down and eat," she said.

Bobby sat down and started eating.

"Rev. Jenkins said he saw you coming out of Carmelo's on Friday night," she said.

"I go in there sometimes," he replied.

"I'm telling you there's nobody in that place that's up to any good," she said. "If I was you, I'd stay as far away from that place as I could."

"Mama, it's a place where a man can go and relax a little after work," Bobby said. "A man needs a little relaxation time."

"You are who you associate out with," she said. "You will do the things that people you associate with do."

"Aw, Mama, you're always worried," he said. "If it's not one thing, it's another."

Bobby finished the last apple pie and got up from the table. He didn't want to hear any more lectures.

"I gotta go," Bobby said. "Idella is waiting on me."

"Wait right here," Hattie said.

"What is it?"

"I got something I want to give you," she said.

She disappeared into the bedroom, then returned moments later.

"What you got?"

She produced a small crucifix.

"I want you to wear this," she said. "It will keep you safe."

"Oh, Mama," he said. "I don't need a cross."

"Yes, you do," she said. "Bend down!"

Reluctantly but obediently, Bobby bent down and allowed her to place the cross around his neck. Then he stood erect again.

"There now," his mother said, patting the crucifix. "That will keep you safe."

"Thanks, Mama," he said. "I got to be going now. Idella is waiting on me. I love you."

"I love you too, baby," she said.

Lazarus

As Bobby walked along Sand River Road, he wondered again what the big job was that Lucky had. Bobby was well aware that Lucky did some illegal things. In fact, Bobby had participated in some of them. Twice, over the past six months, he and Lucky had taken the skiff out to the Gulf Stream to meet the bootleg boat from Fort Lauderdale. The skiff, a small, fast boat owned by Carmelo, was kept at a second marina he owned on the Indian River. Lucky liked to use the skiff for special jobs because it was fast and very maneuverable in the open ocean. This second marina was actually a safe house where the bulk moonshine was stored and rebottled. Once rebottled, some of the shine went to Carmelo's marina on Coast Trail, but most of it was delivered to the *bolitas* joints and cathouses in Blue Springs, Orange City, and points west. During the first trip, Bobby and Lucky had transferred fifty gallons of shine to the safe house and, on the second, they had moved seventy gallons. Both times, Lucky paid him fifty dollars for his work and gave him five pints of shine for his own use. Now, Bobby wondered what Lucky was going to pay him twenty-five hundred dollars to do. *It must be big, really big*, Bobby thought.

Twenty minutes later, when Bobby arrived home, Idella was nowhere to be seen. After changing clothes, he grabbed the can of tar and a homemade ladder and climbed up on the roof. Once the hole was patched, he repaired the door on the chicken coop. By then, it was almost two and he walked to the ocean. The tide was going out and, within an hour, he knew the water would be calm. He decided to go fishing.

Back at the house, Bobby went into the shed and pulled out his fishing tackle and oars. With those in hand, he started to the beach. At only ten feet wide, the shed was too small to shelter his aluminum boat, which was twelve feet. As a result, Bobby kept the boat hidden in the thick undergrowth between the house and the ocean. Moments later, he stopped in front of a stand of pygmy palms where blue morning glory and scuppernong vines had grown over the tops and created a thick canopy. Quickly, he ducked inside the canopy and started to manhandle the boat out of the foliage. As he did, a cotton blanket fell out of the boat. Some nights, if he and Idella were fighting, he would come sleep under the boat. Once the boat was on its bottom, Bobby placed the tackle, oars, and bait inside the hull. Then, using a rope tied to the bow, he started to pull the boat along the sandy path to the ocean.

At the point when the path met the beach, there was an enormous forest of sea oats. The slender, reedy plants stretched from the high tide point at the beach some thirty yards inland and, years before, Bobby had dubbed the place "Sea Oats Cove." To the north, some forty yards away and hidden within the sea oats, sat a small, tarpaper shack. This was where Lazarus Jones lived with his grandmother.

Once he arrived at the beach, Bobby saw Lazarus crabbing in the tidal pools.

"Lazarus!" Bobby called. "What you doing?"

"Trying to catch a mess of crab for me and Grandma."

"Having any luck?"

"I got four or five," Lazarus said. "I need about twenty."

"Yeah, I know," Bobby said. "Takes lots of crabs to get a meal. You want to go fishing with me?"

"Hot dog!" he replied. "I'd love to go."

Ten minutes later, Bobby was plying the oars as the small boat edged along the coastline toward Coronado Inlet. Bobby had known Lazarus for over eight years. At age thirteen, Lazarus lived with his grandmother in the tarpaper shack overlooking the inlet. Clifford, who was Lazarus's uncle, said they had a meager existence. Lots of times, if Bobby came in with a good catch, he would give a shrill whistle toward the shack and the teenager would come running to the beach and Bobby would share his catch.

Finally, Bobby brought the boat through the inlet, then negotiated it into a small cove where he tied up to a cypress stump. Bobby baited two lines for himself and one for Lazarus. As they waited quietly, Lazarus took half of a paperback book from his pocket and started reading.

"What you reading?" Bobby asked.

"*The Gathering Storm*," Lazarus said, "by Winston Churchill."

"Winston who?"

"Winston Churchill," Lazarus replied. "He was prime minister of England during World War II."

Bobby laughed.

"You only got half a book," he said.

"Yeah," Lazarus said. "That's how I found it down in the trash pile. Somebody threw away a whole box of books. I got *Ferdinand the Bull* and *Snow White* and a bunch of books about math and science. There was a copy of *Les Miserables*, but I couldn't read it."

"Why not?"

"It was in French."

"Oh…" Bobby replied.

They watched their lines for several minutes.

"There are lots of good stories in history," Lazarus said finally.

"Like what?" Bobby said.

"One of my favorites is Hannibal," Lazarus said. "Hannibal was this black man from Carthage who lived just after Christ and took his elephants and armies across the Alps to attack Rome. He knew how to use the elephants as weapons."

"How'd he do that?" Bobby asked.

"The soldiers would tie swords to the elephants' trunks, then get them drunk on rice wine."

"Get an elephant drunk?"

"Yeah," Lazarus continued. "Then they would send these drunk elephants charging into the enemy lines. Of course, no man could withstand a drunk elephant charging at him, swinging a sword on his trunk."

"Yeah," Bobby said with a big laugh. "I can see that."

"Only problem was the elephants couldn't tell the difference between the enemy and Hannibal's own troops and sometimes the drunk elephants would attack Hannibal's soldiers."

"What did they do then?"

"There was a guy that sat on the elephant's head," Lazarus said. "If an elephant attacked Hannibal's own troops, his job was to stick a knife in the top of the elephant's head and kill it."

"They had to kill the elephant to save their own troops?" Bobby asked, laughing again.

"That's right," Lazarus said.

Bobby continued to laugh, then doubled over at the thought of the drunk elephants.

"That's a great story," he said.

"Like I told you," Lazarus said. "There are some great stories in history."

They remained quiet, watching their lines.

"What you planning on doing when you're grown up?" Bobby asked.

"Well, I don't really know," Lazarus said. "I can tell you what I'd like to do."

"What's that?"

"I want to be an educated black man. I'd like to go to college and be a history professor."

Bobby peered at him.

"It takes money for that," Bobby said. "Lazarus, you're colored like me. Where you going to get the money to do something like that?"

"I don't know," Lazarus replied. "I got a friend of mine going to the Negro college up in Daytona Beach. He's studying to be a math teacher."

"Where'd he get the money for college?"

"His father owns an insurance company."

"See!" Bobby said. "He's got money. It takes money to go to college."

Lazarus inhaled thoughtfully.

"Yeah," he said finally. "I guess you're right. It's just sort of a dream of mine."

"I don't know anything about college," Bobby said finally. "All I know is fishing and making cane syrup."

"You told me one time you liked to read," Lazarus said.

"Yes," Bobby replied. "I do like to read, but I can never seem to find the time."

"You don't know how smart you are until you start reading," Lazarus said. "That's what my teacher says."

Bobby smiled. He could see the truth of the statement.

***

After two hours, they had caught three small grouper and two redfish. Bored, and shoulders sore from tugging on the oars, Bobby took the boat back down the coast. Before he said good-bye, he gave Lazarus two of the fish.

"Me and Grandma gonna eat good tonight," the teenager said. "Thanks, Bobby!"

As Bobby watched Lazarus race through the sea oats toward the tarpaper shack, his heart went out to the teenager. Lazarus attended the Carver school for Negroes in Wakoola Springs. Clifford said, when Lazarus was a baby, his parents were involved in an armed robbery in Blue Springs. In a shootout with police, his father had been killed and his mother was later sentenced to prison. As a result, Lazarus was sent to live with his grandmother. Although the grandmother had a garden and chickens, they lived hand-to-mouth. Clifford said, after the grandmother told school authorities she couldn't afford to pay for Lazarus's school lunches, he went to the school every year and paid for them.

***

The following morning, which was Thursday, Bobby was up at daybreak. Once he was washed and had fresh overalls, he grabbed a double-bitted axe and a yard rake out of the shed and headed down Sand River Road. He was off work at the sugar mill and was headed to the church to clear off his father's grave. Twenty minutes later, he arrived at the church, then made his way through the headstones to his father's grave. A small live oak tree, maybe fifteen feet tall, had blown down and knocked over the headstone. His father had asked to be buried under a tree. He said the Florida sun got miserably hot in late August and he wanted to spend the ages in the shade. Quickly, Bobby set aside the three plastic blue flowers atop the grave, then started chopping the small tree into sections. Twenty minutes later, he carried each section to the edge of the cemetery and tossed it into the thick silver palmetto undergrowth.

As he raked off the grave, his thoughts wandered back to memories of his father. In 1931, the year Bobby was born, his parents were living and working on a cotton plantation near Greenville, Mississippi. In the summer of 1932, the Mississippi River flooded its banks, inundated the plantation, and Bobby and his parents lived eight months in a government-sponsored relief camp for flood victims. At the camp, his father befriended a Cuban itinerant farmer worker who was en route to Florida. Together, they pooled their resources and bought a car.

Upon arrival in Wakoola County, Bobby's father quickly found work in the potato fields and orange groves and his mother took a job as a housekeeper for Judge Harold Chillingsworth, a prominent judge in Wakoola Springs, and his wife Margaret. "Miss Margaret," as Bobby called her, was a prominent member of the upper crust in Wakoola Springs. She was vice president of the local Democratic Party, a member of the Garden Club, and a frequent sponsor of charity events.

Over the years his mother worked for the Chillingsworths, Bobby learned to love Miss Margaret. She always made a fuss over Bobby when she saw him, but his favorite memories of her were at Christmas. Each and every Christmas, she would come to the Lincoln home with toys, candy, and cookies. His fondest memories of Christmas were seeing Miss Margaret at their door on Christmas day. Most of all, he remembered the peanut butter cookies she made and brought every Christmas. One Christmas, she had bought Bobby a wind-up toy bulldozer, a set of checkers and dominoes, and some clothes, but the first gift he opened was the tin of peanut butter cookies. During all the years his mother worked for Miss Margaret, Bobby never met her husband.

Now that both parents had meager but steady incomes, they decided to buy a house. After extensive searching, the only property they could afford was a small abandoned dwelling on Sand River Road next door to Clifford. It was owned by the county and had a price tag of four hundred fifty dollars. Once the papers were signed, they settled in and quickly became friends with Clifford and Lucille, his wife at the time.

Now that Bobby's father had some permanency, he decided to seek work outside of the fields. One day, Clifford told Bobby's father that Cunningham Demolition, the company where he worked, had an opening. The owner of the company was a man named Sam Cunningham, a local businessman who dabbled in politics. The next day, Bobby's father appeared at the business with Clifford and was hired on the spot. Over the next eight years, Bobby's father worked with Clifford in the home demolition business. It was decent money and, while they didn't have money for luxuries, they ate well. One day, while tearing down an office building, Bobby's father pushed the company owner to safety when he saw that strong winds were about to bring a brick wall down on top of him. Afterward, Sam Cunningham never forgot the incident and credited Bobby's father with saving his life.

Then, one day in 1949, the business owner announced he had been elected sheriff of Wakoola County and he was closing down the business. That meant Bobby's father would have to return to work in the fields. In the early spring of 1950, Bobby's father was plowing during a light rain when a lightning strike caused the mule to bolt and Bobby's father was dragged almost fifty yards before the other workers could get control of the mule. When the mule bolted, the line twisted around his father's neck and he was killed instantly.

Now the grave had been raked clean. Bobby lifted the marble headstone and set it upright on its base. Then he retrieved the blue plastic flowers and replaced them in the moist soil in the center on the grave. Finally, he carried the leaves and broken limbs to the trash pile at the edge of the cemetery. Then, with the axe over his shoulder and the rake in hand, he turned and started walking back down Sand River Road.

Fight at Carmelo's

On Friday night, when the shutdown whistle blew, Bobby, with Train in tow, left the sugar mill and headed to Carmelo's to meet Pee-Wee. He had his week's pay and was ready to get the little engine.

Once inside, Train went straight to the *bolitas* room while Bobby went looking for Pee-Wee. The place was noisy, crowded, and the smell of smoke, rotgut whiskey, and bathroom sanitizer hung in the air. It was Friday night and a diverse assemblage of migrant workers, Haitian cane cutters, Puerto Rican, Jamaican, and Cuban plowmen as well as hundreds of Mexican crop pickers had their payday and were in town for a good time.

Bobby spent more than thirty minutes plowing through the crowd trying to find Pee-Wee. First, he looked in the restaurant, then in the poolroom. Finally, with no Pee-Wee in sight, Bobby went to the *bolitas* room and found Train picking numbers for the night's drawings. The *bolitas* room was once a storage area at Carmelo's that had been converted to a meeting hall with some seventy theater seats facing a giant blackboard and podium. Carmelo would open a drawing by posting numbers from 1 to 100 on the blackboard, which were up for sale. As each number was sold, he would scratch it off. Upon buying a number, which cost five dollars, the purchaser was given a small piece of paper, which confirmed his number for that drawing. Once all the numbers were sold, one hundred small plastic balls, numbered 1 to 100, were placed inside a canvas bag, shaken, and a winner was drawn. The winner collected four hundred fifty dollars and Carmelo kept the rest. Winnings from a single drawing was more than ten times what the average worker earned in a week.

Train was peering at the blackboard when Bobby took a seat beside him.

"Damn!" Train said. "Fourteen is gone! That's my lucky number."

"Thirty-eight is a lucky number too," Bobby said. "I won with it back last spring."

Train shook his head.

"No," he said. "I never liked that number."

"I thought you told me you already owed Carmelo for losses," Bobby said.

"I do," Train said, peering at the blackboard. "But I got cash tonight and I'm going to win. When I do, I'm paying off all the credits."

Bobby knew how fascinated Train was by the *bolitas* games. Over the years, he had watched Train use all sorts of different criteria to try to select a winning number. The year of his birth, the amount of his weekly pay at the sugar mill, the day of the month, and his shoe size had all been used one time or another to pick a winner. The times he won, he was walking on clouds. The times he lost, which was far more often than he won, he was in the doldrums. It seemed the happiness in Train's life went hand in hand with the gambling. It crossed Bobby's mind to buy a number himself. Maybe he would get lucky. He had won a drawing the previous spring and he and Idella lived good until the money ran out. Since the win, however, he had lost seven or eight separate times. Finally, noting how badly he needed the engine, he decided against it.

Bobby remembered once, during the previous summer, when the game was suddenly shut down. It was a Friday night and players were buying numbers when Carmelo suddenly announced everybody had to leave and there would be no further moonshine or *bolitas* sales. He said players who had already bought tickets should return in two days to get a refund. Quickly, the place emptied and all signs of the moonshine sales disappeared. Thirty minutes after the place was cleared, police, sirens screaming and guns drawn, rushed in to raid the place. Officers said they suspected bootlegging and gambling was taking place on the premises, but Carmelo protested he ran a clean, law-abiding establishment. The officers looked around and, satisfied that nothing illegal was taking place, left. Bobby wondered how Carmelo knew the place was about to be raided.

***

Two hours later, all of the numbers had been sold and players who had bought numbers were jammed into the smoke-filled room for the big drawing. When Carmelo and Lucky, who often drew the winning number, stepped up on the podium, there was a rousing round of applause. Bobby and Train were at the front of the crowd.

Once the crowd was settled, Carmelo held up a clear plastic jug, which contained the one hundred plastic balls for all to see. The crowd cheered again as Carmelo handed the jug of balls to Lucky. While Carmelo held open a canvas bag, Lucky dumped the balls inside and Carmelo began to shake the bag vigorously. Finally satisfied the balls were sufficiently mixed, Carmelo turned to the players.

"Are you ready?" he asked.

There was a rousing round of "Yes!"

Then, as Carmelo held the bag open, Lucky reached inside and withdrew one of the balls. The crowd waited anxiously as Lucky looked at the number.

"78 is the winner," he announced.

"That's me!!" said a middle-aged Cuban man, holding up a small piece of paper.

"No!!" said a young, very dark Haitian man. "That's me!!"

Carmelo looked at Lucky for an answer.

"Both of you come on up!" Carmelo said. "I want to see your tickets."

Both men stepped forward and presented their tickets. As Carmelo examined them, a hush fell across the crowd.

"You're the winner!" Carmelo said, touching the shoulder of the Cuban man.

"No! I'm the winner!" said the young Haitian. "I'm the one to get the money!!"

"Your number was 73 and you changed it to 78," Carmelo said, glaring at the young Haitian.

"No! No! You lie! You lie!!" the young Haitian shouted. "I make no change!!"

Carmelo, with a wave of his hand, dismissed the Haitian.

"This is the winner!" he said, pointing to the Cuban.

Anger flared across the Haitian's face and he charged the podium to face Lucky and Carmelo.

"You cheat!! You cheat!!" he shouted. "You lie and you cheat!!"

Lucky peered down at the young Haitian.

"What did you say to me?" he said calmly.

"You cheat!! You lie!!" the young Haitian repeated angrily.

A furious expression crossed Lucky's face. Instantly, he stepped off the podium and pulled a pistol from his hip pocket. For a moment, once Lucky was on the *bolitas* room floor, the Haitian stood his ground and put up his fists to fight, but it was too late. Lucky stepped forward and slapped him across the face with the barrel of the pistol. The Haitian touched his face and felt the blood, then he charged into Lucky, but the big Brazilian was too strong for the smaller man. Seconds later, the young Haitian was on the floor and Lucky was atop him, slapping him again and again across the face with the pistol. The Haitian, holding up his arms to ward off the blows, was virtually helpless as Lucky struck blow after blow.

Bobby stepped forward.

"Lucky! Lucky!" Bobby said. "Get up! You're going to kill him!!"

Lucky looked up at Bobby.

"What do you think I'm trying to do?" Lucky replied.

"Come on!" Bobby said. "Get up! He's had enough!"

Lucky stopped. Then, still sitting atop the whipped man with pistol at the ready, Lucky looked down at the Haitian. His face was a bloody mess. Several teeth had been knocked out, blood was streaming from his nose, and there was a huge gash across his forehead.

Lucky, calmer now and satisfied the Haitian was whipped, slowly stood up. He was still holding the pistol.

The Haitian raised himself to a sitting position on the *bolitas* room floor as Lucky glared at him.

"You ever mess with me again, I'll kill you," Lucky said.

The Haitian didn't answer. This silence infuriated Lucky.

Suddenly, the big Brazilian stepped forward and delivered a strong kick into the Haitian's leg.

"Do you understand?" Lucky asked again.

"Yes. I understand," the young Haitian said.

Then, as the others watched, the young Haitian got up.

"Now get out of here!" Lucky said.

Lucky, Bobby, Carmelo, and the other players watched as the young Haitian made his way through the smoke and the crowd to the exit.

Bobby turned to Lucky.

"I'll see you in the morning," he said.

Later, as he walked home, Bobby was sorely disappointed he had not been able to connect with Pee-Wee.

Little Engine

The next morning, which was Saturday, Bobby was back at the marina to help Lucky with the day's charter. When the fishing party arrived, Bobby had everything ready. By nine a.m., Bobby, Lucky, and a party of four were at the "big hole" some four miles offshore, fishing for cobia. Over the next four hours, the party of four men drank beer, ate sandwiches, talked about sports and women, and caught more than forty pounds of fish. There were kings, red snapper, bonita, and cobia. When the *Lady* pulled back into the marina, the party was laughing, joking, and having a good time. It had been a successful charter.

Once the party had left, Bobby swabbed down the deck, put away the rods and reels, and sat down with Lucky to settle up.

"That's another five dollars we'll knock off what you owe me," Lucky said. "We're back to fifty-three dollars again."

"That's right," Bobby said.

Lucky peered at the cross Bobby was wearing.

"Where did you get that cross?"

"My mother gave it to me."

Lucky moved closer.

"That's a nice cross," he said. "You want to sell it?"

"I can't do that," Bobby said. "I got it from my mother."

Lucky studied Bobby for a moment.

"You know, I really need the money you owe me," he said finally. "You got paid yesterday, didn't you?"

"Yeah," Bobby replied. "I got paid, but I need that money to buy the engine. Pee-Wee was supposed to be here last night but never showed."

"It might be another week or two before Pee-Wee shows up here again," Lucky said. "He's a busy man!"

"Look," Bobby said. "I'll pay you what I owe you. I always do, don't I?"

"Yeah, I know," Lucky said, "but I need that money now. I've got to have the engine overhauled in the *Lady*. I've got dock fees to pay. I really need that money."

"You're going to have to give me some time," Bobby said.

"That what you been saying for the past six months," Lucky said. "I need my money."

Bobby inhaled and shook his head resignedly. He knew Lucky was right; Lucky had been patient with him about the money. Maybe he could give him part of it.

"Okay!" Bobby said. "I'll give you twenty of what I owe you. Will that be okay for a while?"

"That will help," Lucky said. "Give me twenty dollars and I'll let the rest ride for a while."

Reluctantly, Bobby reached in his pocket, unfolded a twenty-dollar bill, and handed it to Lucky.

"Thanks," he said. "You still owe me thirty-three dollars."

"I know! I know!" Bobby said. "I'll get it soon as I can."

Lucky fell silent.

"You sure you're not interested in this big job?"

"You never told me what it is."

"All I want you to do is run the skiff," Lucky said. "That's all you have to do..."

Bobby was ready to end the conversation.

"Let me think about it," Bobby said.

Ten minutes later, Bobby and Lucky were walking back along the wooden walkway to the marina restaurant. On Saturdays, there was always a throng of black men gathered at the marina entrance. Some were seeking work, others were waiting to clean fish, while still others were waiting to play *bolitas* or just loitering. As Bobby and Lucky strode along the walkway, Bobby suddenly heard a voice he recognized.

"Hey!" he heard the voice shout.

Bobby peered toward the marina entrance. There he saw Pee-Wee, his minions behind him, addressing the crowd of black men gathered at the entrance. He was gesturing violently as he talked.

"When you niggers see me coming," he said angrily, "get the hell out of my way!!"

The crowd of black men, some twenty or thirty strong, slowly parted to make room for the little man and his minions. Then, with a ridiculous swagger, Pee-Wee adjusted the butt of the pistol in his shoulder holster so it bulged higher under his coat for all to see. Lustily swinging his arms, he and the other two headed toward the restaurant.

"You niggers going to have to learn who's boss around here," he said as he swaggered past them.

Quickly, Bobby rushed forward to get the little man's attention.

"Mr. Pee-Wee, sir?" Bobby called. "Mr. Pee-Wee, sir?"

The little man stopped, adjusted his thick glasses, then looked at Bobby.

"Ain't you the nigger I talked to about that engine?"

"Yes, sir," Bobby said.

"You got the money?"

"Can you give me just a minute?" Bobby asked.

"You got the money or ain't you?" Pee-Wee pressed. Pee-Wee laughed and shook his head in disgust. "You niggers never have any money," he said. "If you get the money, I'll be inside."

Bobby watched as Pee-Wee and the others turned and went inside the restaurant.

Bobby turned to Lucky. There was urgency in his face.

"You got to help me with this," Bobby said. "I really need this engine. Can you let me have that twenty back so I can get the engine?"

Lucky shook his head.

"Holy Christ!" Lucky said. "Why do we have to keep going over this? You already owe me!"

"Look, I've always been there for you," Bobby said. "Can't you help me out with this?"

"I can't just keep giving you money when there is no chance I'm going to get it back."

Bobby shook his head in frustration.

"Tell you what..." Lucky said finally. "Let me hold that cross and I'll let you have the twenty dollars back. But I'm holding the cross until I'm paid in full."

"I can't be pawning this cross to you," Bobby said. "My mother gave it to me."

Lucky shook his head.

"That's the only way I can give you the money," Lucky said. "I got to have some insurance."

"I can't give you this cross!" Bobby said.

"No cross! No money!" Lucky said firmly.

Bobby inhaled; he really needed the engine. It would mean plenty of food in the house and it would get Idella off his back.

"All right," he said finally. "Don't look like I got much choice."

He unclasped the chain and removed the cross.

"Here!" he said, handing it to Lucky.

Lucky took the cross and examined it.

"It's really a nice cross," he said. "You'll get it back when you've paid me all the money you owe."

"Okay! Okay!" Bobby said. "Now where's the twenty dollars?"

Lucky pulled a wad of bills from his pocket and handed Bobby a twenty.

"Now you owe me fifty-three dollars again."

"I know! I know!" Bobby said disgustedly. "You'll get your money. You always do."

Happy Days

On the following day, which was Sunday, Bobby was anxious to try out the new motor. That morning, he was up early, had breakfast, and started out the door to the beach.

"You ain't going to church again?" Idella asked

"Nope."

"Yo mama ain't going to be happy," she replied.

"Well, tell her I got to put food on the table."

"Whatever..." Idella replied.

Bobby didn't hear her. He was already out the door.

Ten minutes later, he had the new engine in hand and was lugging it through the palmetto undergrowth. Once he was at the boat, he laid the engine inside, then began pulling the boat over the sand to the beach. When he reached the beach, he shoved the boat into the water, then turned toward the shack on the hill and gave a shrill whistle. Suddenly, Lazarus appeared on the front porch. He waved at Bobby, then came bounding down the hill through the sea oats.

"Bobby!" he called, seeing the engine. "What you got there?"

"Power!!" Bobby said. "Power to push my boat."

"You got a new motor? Hot dog!!" Lazarus said. "It looks like a good one."

"Got a good deal on it," Bobby said. "Want to go out with me?"

"I'd love to," the teenager said.

Lazarus watched as Bobby attached the small engine to the rear of the boat. Then Lazarus pushed the boat into the water and hopped in. Moments later, Bobby fired up the engine. The whine of the little engine was music to Bobby's ears. As he turned the boat away from the beach, he knew exactly where he wanted to go. About a mile north of Coronado Inlet, Bobby knew a small cove that had a huge colony of blue crabs.

He hadn't been there in almost a year, but now that he had the engine, now was the time. The tide was going out, so he knew there would be shallow water in the cove.

As they cruised up the coast, Lazarus turned to Bobby.

"Where we going?" Lazarus said.

"To my secret blue crab hole," Bobby said. "Should be lots of blue crabs."

"Can I get some?" Lazarus asked.

"Of course," Bobby said.

"Hot dog!" Lazarus replied with a big smile.

Bobby smiled at Lazarus's childish excitement. He liked Lazarus. He liked being around him because he knew the teenager looked up to him.

Twenty minutes later, Bobby was easing the boat along the coast. He knew he was in the vicinity of the cove, but over the past year, the new undergrowth of mangrove had created a thick wall of foliage, which made it much harder to find.

"There is a small inlet somewhere here," he said. "I'm gonna ease the boat along the edges of this mangrove. Take the paddle and pull back the mangrove and let's see if we can find it."

Lazarus did as he was ordered. He loved the sense of adventure he got when he was around Bobby.

Moments later, as the boat eased along the wall of mangrove, Lazarus would intermittently thrust a paddle into the foliage, trying to find an opening. After some ten minutes, he had made seven or eight attempts.

"Here it is," Lazarus said finally.

Instantly, Bobby headed the boat into the shallow cove. Inside, the small cove was mostly open water with intermittent clumps of rotted cypress trunks. Bobby knew exactly where he was going. Moments later, he eased the boat into a sandy point that jutted out from the mangrove. Then he shut down the engine and let the boat drift into a fallen cypress tree. Once the boat was tied up, Bobby peered into the crystal clear water. In a narrow indentation some two feet down, Bobby could see the bottom crawling with blue crabs. Thousands of blue crabs.

"Lazarus," he said. "Come look at this."

Lazarus came to the end of the boat and peered where Bobby was pointing.

Suddenly, his eyes were as big as saucers.

"Holy moly!" he said. "I never seen so many blue crabs in my life. There's thousands of them. Why, we could eat blue crab for two or three months."

"Let's take fifty each," Bobby said. "We'll save some for later."

Over the next thirty minutes, they scooped blue crabs out of the indentation. Finally, the bottom of the boat was covered with more than one hundred of the blue mollusks.

"You don't guess all these crab will sink the boat, do you?"

Bobby laughed.

"No," he said. "They're not that heavy."

Finally, Bobby motioned they had enough.

"Come on," he said. "Let's go!!"

Moments later, they were cruising back south along the coast.

"One of these days, I'm going to have my own boat," Lazarus said. "I'll be able to go up and down this coast like it was nothing."

"Where you going to get the money for a boat?" Bobby said.

"When I'm an educated black man," Lazarus replied, "I'll have lots of money."

Bobby smiled and shook his head.

"I wish you luck," Bobby said.

Moments later, they were back at the beach in front of the shack where Lazarus lived. Bobby took a small burlap bag from the boat's storage compartment and filled it with crabs, then handed it to Lazarus.

"Thanks!" the teenager said, taking the bag. "Bobby, you know you're the best friend I got."

"I feel the same way," Bobby said.

Lazarus turned and started the long walk to the shack.

As Bobby watched Lazarus lugging the burlap bag through the sea oats, his heart went out to him. He remembered how hard he and his mother had it after his father died, but it was minimal compared to how Lazarus lived. Bobby always enjoyed his time with Lazarus.

***

It was early afternoon when Bobby arrived back at the house. He knew Idella would be back from church. As he approached the house, carrying a huge burlap bag over this shoulder, Idella met him at the back door.

"What you got?" she asked.

"Lots of good eating," he said.

Bobby hefted the burlap bag onto the floor of the back porch and opened it. Idella looked inside.

"Oh, my lord," she said. "We going to be eating crab tonight."

She stood, went to Bobby, and kissed him.

"I love you," she said.

Then she turned toward the kitchen.

"I'm going to put on a big pot of boiling water and make some crab sauce," she said. "Give me about an hour."

They had a wonderful night. First, they ate all of the blue crabs they could hold. Then they made love again and again. Finally, they stopped and talked about their lives together. She told him she wanted to be married at some point and have children with him. He said that was in the future. Finally, sleepy from all the crab and tired from the lovemaking, they went to sleep. As Bobby drifted off to sleep, he wondered again what the big job was that Lucky had.

Shakedown

A week passed. During that time, Bobby worked two days at the sugar mill and did one charter trip for Lucky. It was a good week. He and Idella hadn't had a single fight. There had been plenty of food in the house and she was happy. On Thursday night, he and Idella went to his mother's house for dinner. Before they left, his mother asked about the cross and he lied and told her he had left it at home. The following morning, he left the house early to put in a day at the sugar mill. Over the next ten hours, he put a total of twenty-two loads of cane through the rollers. When the shutdown whistle blew, he was glad the day was over. Not only was it Friday, but it was payday. After the machines were shut down, the men gathered to collect their pay. One by one, each employee received their pay envelope from the foreman, then signed a sheet that confirmed the payout. When Bobby got his, there was forty-one dollars in cash inside.

After Bobby, Train, and Clifford had collected their pay, they were walking back along Sand River Road toward Palm Harbor when the black Cadillac Bobby had seen a week earlier at Carmelo's stopped in front of them. The three watched curiously as Pee-Wee got out of the Cadillac and approached them. His minions followed.

"Train!" Pee-Wee said. "Carmelo wants his money. I know you got paid today."

"I know I owe Carmelo," Train said. "He'll get his money!"

"That's not good enough," Pee-Wee said. "He wants it now. Where's your payday?"

As Train and Pee-Wee spoke, Jaybird walked around behind Train.

"I can't give you my payday," Train said. "I got rent to pay."

"No! No!" Pee-Wee said, pulling out a pistol. "That money belongs to Carmelo. Either give it up or we'll take it."

"No!" Train said. "I need my money!!"

Instantly, Jaybird grabbed Train from behind and held him in a chokehold. Train was a head shorter than his aggressor and was virtually helpless in his grasp. Then, as Bobby and Clifford watched, Dooley stepped forward and started rifling through Train's pockets.

"What are you guys doing?" Bobby said. "You can't treat Train like that!"

Pee-Wee turned on Bobby.

"Keep your mouth shut, nigger," Pee-Wee ordered, training the pistol on Bobby. "One more word and you won't be using that engine I sold you ever again."

Bobby glared angrily at Pee-Wee.

"You can't do this to Train," Bobby said again.

"Didn't you hear me?" Pee-Wee said. "You want me to blow yo brains all over them palm trees?"

Bobby didn't reply.

"Answer me!" Pee-Wee shouted, cocking the pistol and training it on Bobby's head.

Bobby knew it was time to back down.

"No, sir!!" Bobby replied.

"Then stay out of this!" Pee-Wee said.

By now, Dooley had finished rifling through Train's pockets and found his pay envelope. He handed it to Pee-Wee.

"Let's see what we got here," the little man said, opening the envelope.

He withdrew the money and counted.

"There's forty-eight dollars here," Pee-Wee said. "Carmelo says you owe him forty-five."

Train didn't answer.

"Well, if you can't decide, I can," Pee-Wee said, stuffing the owed amount in his pocket and throwing the remainder on the ground.

"All right," Pee-Wee said. "Let him go!"

The three started back to the Cadillac. Then Pee-Wee stopped and turned.

"You boys have a good day!" Pee-Wee said with a laugh.

Then, as Bobby, Train, and Clifford watched, Pee-Wee and his minions returned to the black Cadillac. Moments later, the engine started and the sedan sped off down the highway.

Bobby looked after the black Cadillac as it disappeared.

"One of these days, somebody is going to kill those guys," Bobby said. "It's just a matter of time."

Train laughed.

"You don't mess with those guys," Train said. "They do whatever they want. If they want to kill you, they just drive up and blow you away. No warning!! They just come up on you like a hunter does a rabbit and start shooting. And nothing ever gets done about it."

"I never heard of anything like that," Bobby replied.

"That's because you don't know what really goes on in this county," Train said.

"What you talking about?" Bobby asked.

"These people own all of the politicians," Train replied. "If the little man or one of his goons had shot and killed one of us, nothing would have ever been done about it."

"You mean to tell me Pee-Wee and his boys go around killing people and nothing ever gets done?"

"That's right," Train said. "If they go out and kill a man, they never face trial."

Bobby peered disbelievingly at Train.

"They don't do that kind of stuff anymore," Bobby said. "Back in the old days, maybe, but not anymore."

"To hell they don't," Train said. "Pee-Wee and his boys own all of the politicians. Remember three months ago when the cops came into Carmelo's? Thirty minutes earlier, Carmelo had run everybody out and shut down the shine and *bolitas.*"

"I remember," Bobby said. "I wondered how that happened."

"If the police get a warrant to raid a gambling joint," Train said, "there is a judge who calls the joint owner ahead of time and tells them the raid is coming."

"A judge that warns them?" Bobby asked. "Who's the judge?"

"I don't know," Train replied. "I don't want to know. If I did, I'd probably be a dead man."

The three walked quietly.

Bobby looked at Clifford.

"Train is right," Clifford said. "These guys ain't nobody to mess with. The further away you stay away from them, the better off you will be."

Bobby scoffed.

"You guys get scared at the least little thing," he said. "I ain't afraid of them. You give me an army .45 and two clips and I'll take on the whole bunch of them."

Train laughed.

"They'll blow you to kingdom come before you get off a shot."

Bobby looked at Train. His eyes were hard.

"There's a side to me you don't know," he said.

"What's that?"

"I learned to kill in the army," Bobby said. "That's what they trained me to do."

"You ain't going to kill me, are you?" Train asked.

Bobby laughed.

"You know better than that," he said. "You're my friend."

Train put his arm around Bobby's shoulder and hugged him.

They continued walking.

"Can I borrow a little from you guys to make it through the week?"

"Not me," Bobby said. "It's been real tight with me lately."

Train turned to Clifford.

"What about you?" he asked.

Clifford reached into his pocket and handed Train a five-dollar bill.

***

Twenty minutes later, Bobby had arrived at his house. As he approached, he could see Idella waiting on the front porch. As he started across the yard, he could see her eyes following his every step. He knew there was going to be trouble.

"Hey, baby!" he said.

Her face screwed up in a scowl.

"Don't 'Hey, baby' me," she said. "Why didn't you pay the rent last month?"

"Why you asking me that?"

"Because Mr. Phillips was by here today to collect the rent."

Bobby inhaled.

"Well, you know money has been short lately and…"

"Don't give me that song and dance," she interrupted. "You lied to me!! You told me the rent was paid!!"

Bobby shook his head.

"I don't know what to say," he said.

Quickly, he stepped on the porch and strode past her. She followed him into the house.

"I want an answer," she said. "If you can't tell me the truth about things like this, then I don't need to be with you."

"Let me alone," he said. "I got paid today. I'll go over to Wakoola and pay the rent tomorrow."

"That's not the point," she said. "I want to know why you lied to me."

Bobby went into the bedroom and started to change out of his work clothes. She followed him.

"Have you been playing *bolitas* again?"

He hesitated.

"Yes, you have, haven't you?" she said. "You don't have to lie to me again. What you doing throwing our money away like that? Can't you see how crazy it is?"

Suddenly, he turned on her.

"Leave me alone!" he shouted. "Get the hell away from me!!"

His voice reverberated across the room.

She stopped, calmer now. For a long moment, she peered angrily at him, then started out of the room. Suddenly, she stopped.

"One of these days, you going to come home and I ain't going to be here."

Once he had finished changing clothes, he went outside to the shed, grabbed a pint of shine, and headed to the beach. Moments later, he was strolling along the beach, sipping the shine. For a moment, he stopped and watched the incoming tide wash over his bare feet. *Money! Money! Money!* he thought. There was never enough money. It would be nice to not have to worry about money for a while. It seemed that every time he thought he was getting a few dollars ahead, there was always someone there waiting to take it. He remembered the big job Lucky had offered. He wanted to talk to Lucky again.

The Agreement

The following day, which was Saturday, Bobby was back at Carmelo's, looking for Lucky. After he didn't see the big Brazilian in the restaurant or the pool hall, he walked to the docks, where he found Lucky sitting on the deck of the *Lady*, smoking a cigarette.

"Bobby!" he said. "Come aboard."

Bobby made his way along the gangplank and took a seat on the deck across from the Brazilian.

"I want to talk to you about this big job," Bobby said.

"What do you want to know?"

"You never did tell me what it's all about."

"I don't think you're ready for a job like that," he said.

"You don't know what I'm ready for," Bobby said.

Lucky peered at him again.

"Are you really interested?" Lucky asked.

"I wouldn't be asking if I wasn't interested."

"What do you want to know?'

"I want to know what you gonna be doing when we get to Flagler's Point. That's the part you haven't told me."

"You sure you're interested?"

"I told you I was interested," Bobby said. "What you got?"

Lucky inhaled for a long moment, then peered at Bobby. Finally, he spoke.

"When we get to Flagler's Point, I'm going into a house there and bring out a person and put him in the boat. Then I want to take him out to the Gulf Stream."

Bobby peered at him.

"What you going to do when we get to the Gulf Stream?"

"I'm going to throw him overboard."

"You gonna kill him?"

Lucky nodded.

Bobby peered at him, horror on his face.

"I ain't having nothing to do with killing nobody," he said. "I'm not that kind of person. I'll go along and drive the boat, but I'm having no part of killing somebody."

"You didn't have any problem driving the skiff out to meet the bootlegger boat," Lucky said.

"That's different," Bobby said. "If I got caught doing something like that, I would probably have to do some time. If I got caught doing what you are talking about, I'd be in jail forever."

"No," Lucky said. "The truth is you're afraid. You ain't got the stomach for it."

"Don't talk like that to me," Bobby said. "I was on a .50 caliber machine gun in Korea. I killed thousands of men."

"So what's the problem now?"

"That was in war," Bobby said. "It was kill or be killed. I wasn't shooting another man in cold blood. That's different."

Lucky shook his head.

"So what you want to do?" Lucky said. "You may never get another chance like this. Twenty-five hundred dollars is a lot of money. It could change your life."

Bobby inhaled. He knew Lucky was right. He had never had that much money in his entire life. He thought of all the things he could buy. He could pay up the rent a year in advance. Idella could get new living room furniture. She would never again be nagging him about how much food there was in the house. Bobby was tempted. Strongly tempted.

"You could clear off your debt to me in one night," Lucky said. "And still have more than twenty-four hundred dollars in your pocket."

Bobby shook his head with indecision.

"Let me think about it," Bobby said.

"When will I hear back from you?" Lucky asked.

"Tomorrow."

"Okay," Lucky said. "I can wait 'til then. Remember, you can't tell anyone about this."

"You don't have to worry about that," Bobby said. "I know how to keep my mouth shut."

"Okay. Come on," Lucky said. "Let's go down to the restaurant and have a meal. I'm buying. I know you don't have any money. You never do."

***

That night, back at home, Idella wasn't speaking to him or sleeping with him. For the past two nights, he had been sleeping on the couch. This particular night, she had made dinner and left him to eat alone. Once he was finished, he went to the shed, grabbed a bottle of shine, and went to the beach. As he walked along the strand, the tide was bringing in dead jellyfish and clumps of blackened seaweed. Absently, he kicked the seaweed with his bare feet. Maybe he should take Lucky up on his offer. It was a lot of money. Maybe Lucky was right. It would be the chance of a lifetime. Maybe it would be worth it to get Idella off his back. If he had that much money, maybe she would quit nagging. He would give anything on this earth to get Idella off his back about money. He decided he would take Lucky's offer.

The following morning was Sunday. When Bobby awoke, he dressed, ate, and went straight to Carmelo's. Through the plate glass window in front of the restaurant, he could see Lucky sitting at a table, smoking a cigarette. Moments later, he was inside.

"Can we talk for a minute?" Bobby said.

"Sure," Lucky said. "Sit down."

"No, I mean privately."

"Come on," Lucky said. "We'll go to the *Lady*."

Ten minutes later, they were seated on the deck of the *Lady*.

"Let me see if I got this straight," Bobby said. "You want me to take the skiff up to Flagler's Point."

"That's right," Lucky said. "I want to go to a house on the beach. Then I want you to wait for me while I go into the house and bring someone out."

"Now I ain't having nothing to do with killing somebody," Bobby said.

"Don't worry about it," Lucky said. "All you've got to do is run the boat and I'll take care of everything else. Just like it was a charter."

Bobby studied the big Brazilian for a long moment.

"When do I get my money?"

"When the job is finished."

"How much will I get?"

Lucky took out a pencil.

"As of right now, you owe me fifty-three dollars," Lucky said, doing the math. "When the job is finished, you'll get $2447.00. To be fair, I'll round it off to $2450.00."

Bobby took a deep breath. He couldn't imagine having that much money.

"And the cross," Bobby said. "I want the cross back."

"When the job is finished, you'll get the cross back."

Bobby put his hand to his forehead, then peered out across the marina. He was about to make a decision that could affect all of the rest of the days of his life. Part of him was fearful. Another part of him was glad to have the opportunity to get Idella off his back.

He turned back to Lucky.

"So do we have a deal?" Lucky asked.

"We got a deal," Bobby replied. "But remember one thing, I ain't having nothing to do with killing nobody."

"Don't worry," Lucky said. "All you got to do is run the boat."

"One more question," Bobby said.

"What's that?"

"Who wants this person dead?"

Lucky smiled.

"You don't need to know that," Lucky said. "Just carry out your end of the deal and everything will be fine."

"When do you want to do it?"

"It will have to be a Saturday night," Lucky said. "Not sure when, but it will be a Saturday night. I'll let you know. Then we have a deal?" Lucky asked.

"We have a deal," Bobby said.

Lucky offered his hand.

Bobby shook it.

***

On Thursday of the following week, Lucky had another charter trip. It was four hours and there were six in the party, including two women. It was an uneventful charter. They had caught around thirty pounds of fish, mostly red snapper, snook, kings, and some small grouper. Once the charter group had left and the *Lady* was scrubbed down, Lucky sat down with Bobby on the deck.

Lucky lit a cigarette.

"The big job will be this Saturday night," he said, taking a deep drag. "We can't have any slipups. Get a good night's sleep the night before. I'll have all the things we need."

"Anything you want me to bring?" Bobby asked.

"Just yourself," Lucky replied. "Have a clear head and be ready to go. I'll meet you here at ten."

"I'll be here," Bobby said.

Murders

Promptly at ten the following Saturday night, Bobby met Lucky at the dock and they boarded *Lucky's Lady*. Ten minutes later, with Bobby at the helm, they were cruising up the coast to Coronado Inlet, then into the Indian River. They were going to the safe house to get the skiff. The safe house was a former marina on the Indian River where Carmelo stored the bulk of the moonshine from the "whiskey boat" until it was ready for distribution. As the boat neared the darkened building, Bobby shut down the engine and the big charter boat nudged the dock. Once the boat was tied up and they were on the dock, they heard a voice.

"Lucky?"

It was Javier, the middle-aged Cuban man who was the guard at the safe house.

"Javier!" Lucky answered. "It's me."

"I've been waiting on you."

Wasting no time, Lucky led Bobby around the side of the building to a skiff, a 22-foot long launch with a 90-horse Thompson engine, which was listing in the water. The vessel was fast and very maneuverable in the open ocean.

Twenty minutes later, with Bobby at the helm, the skiff passed through the inlet and headed south along the coast. High in the sky, a full moon illuminated the open ocean; there was a slight breeze from the southeast and the water was smooth as glass. As the boat sliced through the water, Lucky took out a pint of bonded whiskey, took a swig, then handed the bottle to Bobby. Lucky checked the pistol in his belt.

"The house we're going to has a yellow light on the dock," Lucky said. "It's about four miles. You'll see it."

Lucky scanned the shoreline as the skiff skimmed through the quiet water. For several minutes, the only sound was the whine of the outboard engine. Lucky's eyes were trained on the docks along the coast. Bobby knew they were nearing Flagler's Point.

"There it is!" Lucky said, pointing to a dock in the darkness. "Take her in here to the dock with the yellow light."

Bobby swung the boat toward shore. In the moonlight, Bobby could see the silhouette of a two-story beach cottage against the night sky. As he guided the boat to the dock, he felt the bottom of the boat bumping the bottom.

"It's shallow in here," Bobby said.

"I know," Lucky replied, "but we don't have any choice."

Moments later, the skiff pulled alongside the dock. Lucky tied up the front of the boat while Bobby secured the stern. Quickly, Lucky opened a storage compartment and withdrew a large paper bag. He took out a roll of tape, a length of rope, and a pair of police handcuffs. Lucky checked the pistol in his belt, then stepped off of the boat and onto the wooden dock.

"Wait here," he said.

Bobby could hear Lucky's footsteps as he tromped across the wooden dock toward the house. Moments later, a light came on at the back of the house, the door opened, and Bobby could see the silhouette of Lucky's hulking form as he talked to a man. Then the door opened and Lucky went inside. A light illuminated in the kitchen, then in an upstairs room. Bobby waited. Five minutes, then ten minutes passed.

Then Bobby heard Lucky's voice in the darkness.

"Go on!" Lucky was saying. "Go on or I'll kill you."

Then he heard a woman's voice.

"Stop! Stop!!" the woman begged. "You're hurting my arm."

"You do what I say or I'll kill you," Lucky said.

"You're an animal," the woman said. "No better than a dog!"

"Shut up!" Lucky said. "Come on!"

Suddenly, the woman screamed.

"I told you to shut up!" Lucky said.

Then, just as suddenly, there was a moan and the screaming stopped.

"You son-of-a-bitch!" said a man's voice.

Then Bobby heard footsteps and a shuffling sound on the dock. In the moonlight, he could make out the silhouette of Lucky and another man moving down the dock toward the boat. They stopped. Lucky was securing the man to one of the posts on the dock.

"You make any sound," Lucky said, "and I'll kill the woman."

Then Lucky went back toward the house.

Moments later, he appeared at the boat carrying an unconscious woman. Then he stepped into the boat, laid the woman in the hull, and went back to the dock. Seconds later, Lucky appeared again. This time, he was pushing the man along the dock toward the boat. Now Bobby could see that the man's hands were cuffed in front of his body.

"Why are you doing this?" the man asked.

"Shut up and go on!!" Lucky said, pushing the man along the dock toward the boat.

"Why? Why?" the man asked again.

They had reached the boat.

"Get in!" Lucky said. "Get in or I'll kill you!"

The man resisted and Lucky roughly shoved him into the boat. Once onboard, Lucky seated the man on top of one of the storage compartments, then knelt over the woman. Bobby watched as he taped her mouth shut. Finally, Lucky untied the boat.

"Let's go!" he said.

Bobby fired up the engine. As he slowly maneuvered the boat away from the dock, he could feel the foot of the engine dragging on the shallow, sandy bottom. Once the skiff was clear of the dock, Bobby opened up the engine and headed eastward. Lucky had instructed Bobby to take the boat to the Gulf Stream.

"What are you going to do with us?" the man said.

"None of your business," Lucky said.

Bobby's heart was racing as he guided the skiff eastward. For some fifteen minutes, the only sound was the whirring of the engine and the sound of the skiff slicing through the water. There was an occasional, muffled, whimpering sound from the woman.

Suddenly, the boat engine sputtered, then gained speed again, then sputtered again, and finally stopped.

Lucky looked at Bobby.

"What happened?" Lucky asked

Bobby peered at the instruments.

"The engine is overheated," he said. "We got sand in the water jackets from that shallow bottom."

"Damn!!" Lucky said. "Try it again."

Bobby spun the engine over several times, but it failed to start.

"Stop! Stop!" Lucky said. "No need to run down the battery. We'll have to let it cool."

Bobby could feel the boat drifting aimlessly in the quiet water. His heart was racing. They hadn't counted on something like this. A delay could cause any number of unforeseen problems. They waited five, then ten minutes.

"What are we going to do?" Bobby asked.

"Check the heat gauge again," Lucky said.

Bobby glanced at the console.

"Still overheated," he said.

"Damn!" Lucky said, shaking his head in frustration. "Let's give it a few more minutes."

All was quiet. Suddenly, the man spoke to Bobby.

"Hey, boy," he said. "If you'll take care of us, I'll give you more money than you could ever dream of. You'll never have to work again."

"Shut up!" Lucky said.

"I could give you more money than you could ever spend, boy," he continued. "All you got to do is save us."

With the back of his hand, Lucky slapped the man full across the face.

"You low-down son-of-a-bitch," the man said. Then all was quiet again.

Now the woman, lying prone in the hull, was slowly coming to life. She moaned, then slowly rolled over and made a muffled sound. The boat drifted and they waited.

"What are we going to do?" Bobby asked.

Lucky didn't answer at first.

"Try it again," he said finally.

"It's still overheated," Bobby said.

"Try it anyway."

Bobby spun the engine over for a full ten seconds, but it failed to start.

"Stop! Stop!" Lucky said.

Then all was quiet again.

"It's a Thompson engine," the old man said. "There is a valve on the side of the foot you can open and the engine will flush out the sand as it turns."

Lucky looked at the old man and laughed.

"By God, I think he's right," Lucky said. "Hand me the flashlight."

Moments later, Lucky tilted the engine forward out of the water so he could see its foot. Lucky laughed, then, taking a screwdriver, he opened the valve on the side of the foot.

"Okay," he said. "Spin it over."

Instantly, rivulets of sandy water started to run down the foot of the engine and, suddenly, the engine roared to life.

Lucky laughed out loud. The sound of his laughter reverberated across the ocean's surface.

"Wonders will never cease," he said. "Let's go!"

Bobby spun the boat around and headed eastward toward the Gulf Stream again.

"You going to continue with this after I helped you get the engine started?" the man asked.

"Looks that way," Lucky said with a laugh.

Ten minutes later, the skiff started to slow and Bobby knew they were nearing the Gulf Stream. He knew the effect of the famous ocean current. Its powerful, swirling eddies were pulling the hull of the vessel northward although he had the bow pointed due east.

"We're here!" Bobby said.

"Shut her down," Lucky said.

The engine stopped. Suddenly, the woman let out a blood-curdling scream. Somehow, she had removed the gag. Lucky moved toward her.

"Put a light over here," Lucky ordered. "I can't do this in the dark."

Bobby grabbed a flashlight and trained it on the couple, then he recoiled in horror when he saw the woman's face.

"Miss Margaret?" Bobby blurted out in horror. "Miss Margaret?"

He couldn't believe what he was seeing. The woman was Margaret Chillingsworth, the woman his mother had kept house for all those years. Suddenly, his heart leapt into his mouth.

"Oh, my God," he said. "Lucky, I can't do this!"

"What do you mean?"

"This is Miss Margaret," Bobby said. "This woman has been like a mother to me."

The woman sat up and peered at Bobby.

"Who is that?" she said.

In the overspill of the flashlight, she could make out Bobby's face.

"Bobby? Bobby Lincoln?" she said. "What are you doing here?"

"Oh, my God," Bobby said.

He turned to Lucky.

Lucky's face screwed up in anger.

"This is not the time to be going soft on me," Lucky said. "You agreed to do this. I expect you to live up to your word."

"I know I agreed, but I didn't know this!"

"Bobby, don't do this to me!" the woman said. "I've always been good to you. And your mother! I always helped y'all every way I could."

"Shut up!" Lucky said.

"Please, Bobby," the woman said. "Don't let this man hurt us."

"Keep quiet or I'll blow your head off," Lucky said.

"Bobby," the man said. "Help us! Please help us!!"

Bobby looked at the woman. She was a pitiful sight. She was pleading for her life. He turned to Lucky

"I can't do it," Bobby said, tears in his eyes.

Lucky, his face flush with anger, pulled the pistol out of his belt and pointed it at Bobby.

"You've GOT to do it," he shouted. "Either that or I'll blow your brains all over this boat."

Bobby peered at him calmly for a long moment.

"If you didn't have that gun, I'd kill you," he said.

"Yeah, but I do have the gun and I'm going to kill you along with these two if I have to."

For a moment, all was quiet. The old couple waited for Bobby to make a decision.

"Look!" Lucky said. "Don't be a fool. You're in way too deep to get out now! You're already an accessory to kidnapping. That's thirty years. It's all or nothing now."

Bobby inhaled. Inside, he wanted to cry. He knew Lucky was right. His involvement was far beyond mere innocence at this point. In fact, as he looked around him, in his own mind, he was already guilty. For a moment, he held his hands to his head to halt his thoughts, but it was too late. He had to make a life-altering decision and he had to make it quick. He could feel his insides shaking with desperation. He knew there was no turning back. He peered across the water, then back at Lucky.

"Where's the bottle?" he asked.

Lucky handed him the bottle.

Bobby took a long swig.

"Come on," he said. "Let's get this over with."

"Bobby! Bobby!" the woman pleaded. "Don't do this to me. Please don't do this!"

"Let me shut her up," Lucky said. Quickly, he went to the woman. She struggled desperately as Lucky, using the roll of tape, gagged her mouth shut again. Although gagged, she was still making muffled sounds. Then, Bobby held her firmly while Lucky fitted diving weights over her shoulders and secured them at her waist.

"Let's throw her overboard," Lucky said.

"No!" Bobby said firmly. "We're not going to throw her. We'll lift her over the side and just slip her into the water."

"Okay! Okay!" Lucky said. "Let's go."

"Oh, honey," the man said pitifully. "Always remember I love you."

The woman made a muffled sound as Lucky and Bobby lifted her over the side of the boat. Then, as Bobby looked away, they released her into the water. Lucky shined the flashlight. For a moment, she flailed her arms to stay afloat, but the diving weights were too heavy for her small body. Quickly, her head went under, there was a chorus of bubbles and, in the clear water, they could see her hair flying above her head as she sank into the depths.

Quickly, they turned and started for the old man.

Suddenly, he jumped over the side of the boat and into the water.

"Son-of-a-bitch!" Lucky said. "Put the light on him!"

Moments later, in the flashlight beam, they could see the man, his cuffed hands making a churning motion in the water and dogpaddling away from the boat.

"Start the engine," Lucky said.

Bobby started the engine and the boat pulled alongside the man. Then Lucky grabbed a wooden paddle from the deck and swung it at the man. He missed as the man swam further away.

"Bring the boat closer!" Lucky said.

Again, Bobby maneuvered the boat close to the man and Lucky, much closer this time, slammed the wooden paddle into the side of his head. Blood appeared on top of his balding head as Lucky reached down and pulled him into the boat. The man, gasping for air, was addled but alive.

Quickly, while Bobby held the man, Lucky fitted a set of diving weights over his shoulders. Then, together, they lifted him over the side and released him into the water. For a moment, they couldn't see him. Lucky searched the water with the light.

"Where did he go?" Lucky said. "Put the light on him."

Bobby trained the light on the water.

"Holy Christ!!" Lucky said with disbelief. "He's swimming! He's swimming with those diving weights. Take the boat alongside him. We got to finish the job."

Bobby fired up the engine and maneuvered it alongside the old man.

Lucky looked for something to strike the man with. He picked up the wooden paddle again and struck the man across the head with a glancing blow. The man was still swimming away from the boat.

"Take it closer," Lucky said.

Bobby spun the helm around to move closer.

"No, forget it!" Lucky said. "Hold the light."

He handed the flashlight to Bobby.

"What you gonna do?" Bobby asked.

"Just hold the light," Lucky said.

Instantly, Lucky turned, went to the boat's console, opened the lid, and pulled out a shotgun.

For a moment, as Bobby trained the flashlight, the old man went under water again.

"Where'd he go?" Bobby asked.

"Give it a moment," Lucky said. "He'll come back up."

Suddenly, the man's head reemerged. He was some twenty feet from the boat.

Bobby held the flashlight and Lucky took careful aim.

Blam!

The shotgun blast rang out across the water.

Suddenly, a giant cloud of crimson-red formed in the water around the old man as his life's blood spilled into the churning salt water. Even after he was shot, his cuffed hands continued an up and down churning motion as if he was trying to stay afloat. This continued for five, maybe ten seconds, then the old man's body went limp and he slowly started sinking. As his head went under, there was a chorus of bubbles, then they watched as the white bald spot on top of his head descended into the depths.

Lucky threw the shotgun into the water.

Then he turned to Bobby.

"It's over," he said. "Let's go back."

***

Twenty minutes later, the skiff was quietly cruising back toward the mainland. Bobby was at the helm. Lucky was smoking a cigarette.

"Now it wasn't all that bad," Lucky said. "Was it?"

Bobby glanced at him, not answering. Then, unable to control himself, he put his head over the side of the boat and started vomiting.

Lucky laughed.

Twenty minutes later, the skiff was back through the inlet and cruising along the Indian River to the safe house. Once the skiff was docked, they boarded *Lucky's Lady* and headed back down the coast to the marina. Twenty minutes later, the *Lady* was docked at Carmelo's and they sat down on the deck to settle up.

Lucky counted out the money.

"That's $2450.00," he said. "That's what I promised."

Lucky handed the money to Bobby.

"What about the cross?" Bobby asked.

"That wasn't part of the deal," Lucky said.

"The hell it wasn't," Bobby said. "Get me that cross!"

Lucky didn't move.

"Get me the God-damn cross!" Bobby shouted.

Lucky looked around to see if anyone had heard Bobby's raised voice. There was no one in sight.

"Okay! Okay! Take it easy," Lucky said. "If you want the cross, you owe me another twenty."

Bobby peeled a twenty-dollar bill off the wad of cash. "Here!"

Lucky took the bill, then turned and ducked into the boat cabin. Seconds later, he emerged with the crucifix.

"Here you go," he said.

Bobby took the cross.

"I'm all cleared up with you now, right?" Bobby said. "All my debts are paid and we're square?"

"That's right!" Lucky said

"That's all I wanted to know," Bobby said, stuffing the wad of cash in his pocket. "I'll see you later."

Monster

As he walked home, Bobby could feel the huge wad of paper money bulging in his pocket. He had never had so much money in his life. He smiled at the thought. Twenty minutes later, back at home, Bobby took forty dollars for rent, then put the wad of cash in a quart fruit jar and buried it in the back corner of the shed. He was going to spend it a little at a time. If he started spreading lots of money around, Idella would get suspicious and start asking questions. He would keep the money a secret and use it only as he needed it. Satisfied the money was safe, Bobby went into the house and went to bed.

It was a fitful night. His mind was racing with thoughts of the deed he had done. After dozing off for some thirty minutes, he suddenly sprang wide awake. He was sweaty, feverish, and trembling. Quickly, he got out of bed, went to the shed, and took a bottle. Finally, after several swigs of the rancid liquid, he returned to bed and dozed off to sleep around four a.m.

***

The following morning, when he awoke, Idella was standing over the bed.

"Bobby! Bobby!" she was saying, "Where were you last night?"

Bobby mumbled incoherently, then turned over.

"You going to church today?"

Bobby raised himself to one elbow and rubbed his eyes. "What time is it?"

"After nine," she said. "You going to church?"

"No, I'm sick," he said.

"You going to church today?"

"No!" he said angrily. "I told you I'm sick."

"You don't have to get mad about it."

"I'm not mad," he said. "I just want to sleep."

"Yo mama's not going to be happy."

Bobby didn't reply. He readjusted his head on the pillow, then went back to sleep.

***

Just after noon, he got out of bed and went to the shed. Somehow, the events of the previous night didn't seem real to him. He wanted to be sure they actually happened. He opened the shed door and pulled back the tarpaulin. For a moment, he dug into the sand, then pulled out the quart fruit jar and saw the wad of hundred-dollar bills inside. It was true, he told himself. Too true. Quickly, he returned the fruit jar to his hiding place and went to the beach.

As he strolled along the beach, he sensed something was now going wrong inside him. Deep inside himself, he sensed the deed he had done was taking on a life of its own. He wasn't sure how or to what degree, but he sensed a monster was calmly lurking in the shadows of his mind. He had not yet seen the full frightful features of this monster's face, but he knew he would in the days ahead.

That afternoon, when he returned back home, Idella was cooking.

"Now I'm fixing ham, mashed potatoes, and green beans," she said. "You can eat when you're ready. I'm going to visit

Aunt Flossie this afternoon. I hadn't seen her in over a month. You want to go?"

"No," he said. "I think I'll go down to the docks."

"Suit yourself," she said. "I'll be back around dark."

***

Once she was gone, Bobby was glad. He sat down and ate, then went back to bed and slept until dark.

When Idella returned that night, she wanted to talk about her aunt's new living room furniture.

"It's really nice," she said. "There's a couch in dark brown and two matching end tables. Do you think we could ever get something like that?"

Bobby looked at her with a scowl.

"I don't care anything about your aunt's new furniture," he said. Quickly, he got up and walked out the door.

"What's wrong with you?" she called after him.

Bobby didn't reply.

***

That night, he walked down Coast Road to Carmelo's. As he drew near, he could see the lights and hear the noise. A jukebox was playing, loud voices wafted across the night air, and couples were going in and out of the restaurant. As always, a crowd of hucksters and loiterers were gathered around the entrance. For some thirty minutes, he stood in the darkness. For a moment, he decided to go in, then he changed his mind. He knew Train was in there gambling and Lucky was sitting with Carmelo. For some thirty minutes, he stood in the darkness, watching the comings and goings. He knew if he went inside, he would see Lucky and he would remember the incidents of the previous night.

Finally, he turned and went back home. As he walked, he wondered where his life would go from here. He wondered if he even had a life after what he had done. He could sense the monster that was slowly taking shape inside him. Back at home, he threw back two stiff shots of shine. Then he went to bed.

***

The following morning, which was Monday, Bobby was up early, had a packed lunch, and was walking down Sand River Road to the sugar mill. Train was happy. He had won twenty-six dollars playing *bolitas* over the weekend. Clifford said President Eisenhower was going to integrate the schools in Arkansas. As Bobby passed his mother's house, he saw her on the front porch reading her Bible. She waved as they passed. At work that day, he put twenty-three loads of cane through the rollers and that afternoon, when the shutdown whistle blew, he, Train, and Clifford were walking back along Sand River Road.

As the trio neared his mother's home, Bobby turned to the others.

"I'm going to visit with my mother," he said.

"See you tomorrow," Clifford said.

When he entered the front door, his mother was seated on the couch in the living room. She looked up.

Upon seeing him, she pulled back.

"Bobby!! What's happened to you?" she asked.

"Nothing," he said.

"Something has happened to you!" she said. "I can see the hurt in your face. Have you been down to that bad place again?"

"No, Mama," he said. "I've got to go."

That afternoon, when he arrived home, Idella was waiting on the porch. She was smiling. He knew she was looking for a romantic night.

"Hey, baby!" she said as he approached. "When you ready to eat?"

"I'm not hungry," he said. "I'm tired."

He brushed past her and went into the house.

She followed him.

"What's wrong with you?" she asked. "Why are you treating me like this?"

She followed him into the bedroom, where he was changing clothes.

"Here I fix your food and I'm waiting on you like a good wife and you run right past me like I don't exist. What's wrong?"

"It's nothing against you," he said. "I'm just tired."

Somehow, he now felt very distant from Idella and had no interest in her. His mind was preoccupied with something else. This preoccupation was becoming more important than anything else in his life.

Lost Soul

On Tuesday, when he awoke, Idella had breakfast prepared. As he ate, she peppered him with questions.

"You going down to the docks today?" she asked.

"I'm going to Wakoola to pay the rent."

"You mean you got money?"

He looked at her. He didn't reply.

"Where'd you get money?"

"A guy tipped me ten dollars on the charter Saturday," he lied.

***

Twenty minutes later, Bobby was on the bus to Wakoola Springs. Once he arrived at his landlord's house, Mr. Phillips, a tall, birdlike man in his late sixties, was working in the yard. When Bobby offered him the forty dollars to pay for the rent, he looked surprised.

"You paying the back rent and six months in advance?" he asked.

"Yes, sir."

"First time you ever did that," he said with a quiet smile. "You come into some money?"

"No," Bobby said, shaking his head. "I just didn't want to worry about it for a while."

"That's fine with me," he said. "I'll get you a receipt."

***

Back at home, Idella was cleaning the house.

"Are you going to the docks today?" she asked.

"Maybe later," he lied.

The last person he wanted to be around was Lucky. He blamed Lucky for what he had done. Deep inside, he felt, if he was around Lucky, he was afraid he might fly mad and try to kill him. Even worse, he didn't want to be around Idella. He was fearful of her questions and her constant probing.

He started out the back door.

"Where you going?" she asked.

He didn't answer. All he wanted was to be alone with his thoughts. Outside, at the shed, he grabbed a bottle, then headed to the beach. Moments later, he was strolling barefoot along the sand, sipping the moonshine. As he walked, his thoughts were coming in giant, tormenting waves. *My God, what have I done? Have I ruined my entire life? What can I do to escape this great darkness growing inside me? Is there any salvation for me?* He wondered about God and the nature of a supreme being. He had heard stories of men who had committed murder, then later found peace through religion.

Many times, he had wondered about the nature of God. Growing up in the church and listening to all of the Biblical stories, he had always pictured God as an old man with a beard who carried a staff and was forever making threats and pronouncements about his power. He laughed at the thought. All of that was like a fairy tale you would read to a little child at bedtime, he thought. These were just stories presented to convince non-believers that they should follow the teachings of the Biblical God. It was propaganda like tyrants used to gain power over their citizens. How could any reasoning person believe such fairy tales? The God Bobby was seeking had to be real. A God you could see, feel, and touch. And the creation as explained in the Bible. How could all of this world be created in seven days? First the earth, then the animals and the birds and the fishes of the sea. How was that possible in just seven days? How could anybody believe that? Again, for Bobby, it was like a fairy tale.

As he walked, he wished he had read more books. Maybe he would have a better understanding of such things. He loved to read, but he never could seem to find the time. He wished he had read more about science. Especially biology. He would have a better understanding of how the earth and the creatures upon it were made. When he was in Korea, he had a master sergeant who always spent weekends in the beer garden reading books about World War II. He could go on for hours and hours about the German retreat from Moscow and Hitler's last days. His hero was General Patton and Bobby loved to listen to him talk about Patton's exploits during the war.

As he walked, the soft, foamy waves washed over his bare feet. The sudden chill of the water across his toes seemed to bring alive a secret part of himself. Nothing gave him peace like the sound of the ocean. The constant grating roar of the incoming tide seemed to drown out all voices and thoughts of humankind and the trappings of their world. He could reach his inner self when he was at the beach.

Over the next hour, he walked from "Sea Oats Cove," where he kept his boat hidden, to the rock jetty at Coronado Inlet. As the incoming tide swept around the jetty and into the inlet, pelicans, seagulls, and ospreys were intermittently diving into the swirling water, feasting on the millions of fish being swept into the inlet. One bird would pluck a prize, then another would give chase to snatch it away. He imagined these birds were similar to human beings who fought ferociously among themselves for each and every tasty morsel. Bobby was in a philosophical frame of mind.

Now he was feeling woozy from the moonshine. As he started back down the beach, his intent was to go back to his home and Idella, but he knew he couldn't make it. After walking some thirty or forty feet, he ducked into the thick canopy of fan palmetto and mangrove and lay down. As he rested his head in the sand, he peered up at the canopy of green above him. His mind was getting foggy. The moonshine was closing in and he was getting sleepy. Sleep would be a welcome relief from his torment. His thoughts were sheer torture. In sleep, he could find peace. *Oh, sweet, sweet sleep,* he thought as he dozed off.

***

When Bobby woke up, it was dark. He had slept three, maybe four hours. He emerged from the undergrowth, then strode back down the beach to his home. The minute he walked in the back door, Idella was furious.

"Where've you been?" she shouted. "You can't tell me when you're going to disappear like that? I was worried sick about you."

"Leave me alone," he said.

She went to him and tried to look into his face. He turned away.

"Bobby," she said, "Look at me!"

He turned away again.

"Something bad has happened to you," she said. "Something really bad. I think you're going crazy."

"Leave me alone," he said. "Just leave me alone."

Newspaper Article

The next morning was Wednesday. As per his routine, Bobby was out of bed at daybreak and, lunch pail in hand, strolling down Sand River Road to the sugar mill. News traveled slowly in Palm Harbor, especially among black folks. Most of the locals got their news from their neighbors, the radio, or the *Wakoola County Clarion*, which was published weekly and appeared on Wednesday.

When Bobby arrived at the boarding house, Train joined him and together they walked down Sand River Road. Ahead, they could see Clifford waiting and reading a newspaper.

"Hey," he called as they approached. "Did you guys see this story in the new *County Clarion*? Judge Chillingsworth and his wife have disappeared. Been gone four days."

At first, Bobby wasn't sure if he heard correctly.

"What?" he asked.

"A local judge and his wife have disappeared," Clifford said. "Nobody has seen them for four days."

Bobby froze. He didn't know what to say.

"I don't know anything about it," he said suddenly. "I don't know nothing about it and I don't want to know nothing about."

Suddenly, he started walking ahead of the other two. After he had walked some twenty feet, he stopped.

"Come on!" he said. "Y'all coming to work or not?"

Clifford and Train looked at one another for an answer.

"I don't know about y'all," he said, "but I'm going to work."

Clifford, shocked at Bobby's response, folded the paper, stuffed it in his hip pocket, and started after Bobby. Train was right behind him.

Moments later, they caught up to Bobby.

"Bobby!" Clifford said. "What's wrong?"

"I don't know nothing about some judge disappearing. I got enough troubles of my own."

Again, Train peered at Clifford for an answer. Clifford shrugged in ignorance. The three walked quietly.

Suddenly, Bobby stopped. Then, as Clifford and Train watched, Bobby stepped off to the side of the road and started vomiting.

"Bobby!" Clifford asked again. "What's wrong?"

"It's nothing," Bobby said. "Something I ate. Come on. Let's go to work."

Train looked to Clifford again for an answer. Clifford shrugged.

***

All that day at work, Bobby kept thinking about Miss Margaret. Clifford's innocent mention of the subject had launched him into an avalanche of memories. All that day, his mind was afire with details of the murders. Again and again, the pitiful image on her face as he and Lucky dropped her into the water took stage center in his mind. When her husband had said for her to remember he loved her, Bobby remembered that she had made a muffled sound, probably to say she loved him too, but the gag would not allow the words. His eyes filled with tears at the thought. That afternoon, when the shutdown whistle blew, Bobby quickly shut down the rollers and, although Train was waiting, started walking down Sand River Road alone.

Fifteen minutes later, as he neared his mother's home, she waved to him and called him over.

"Oh, Bobby," she said. "Have you heard the news? Judge Chillingsworth and Miss Margaret have disappeared. The police thinks they've been kidnapped."

"I heard about it, Mama," he said.

"Who would want to hurt them?" she said. "They were some of the nicest white folks I ever met."

Bobby shook his head.

"I don't know, Mama," he said. "Lots of crazy things in this world. I got to go now."

"Why you in such a rush?" she asked. "Got time for some apple pie?"

"No, Mama," he replied. "Idella is waiting."

***

En route home, Bobby stopped at Waddell's Grocery and bought a copy of the *County Clarion*. When he opened it, there was a huge photo of Judge Chillingsworth on the front page. The glaring headline read: "Judge Harold Chillingsworth, Wife Disappear."

He read the story.

"Wakoola County Circuit Judge Harold Chillingsworth and his wife Margaret, both mainstays in local legal and civic life, have disappeared without a trace, according to the county sheriff's office.

"Chillingsworth, 63, and his wife, 61, were abducted Saturday night from their beach home at Flagler's Point sometime around midnight, according to sheriff's deputies.

"Suspicions were aroused when two handymen, who went to the house Sunday morning to repair a deck, reported finding no one home and a trail of blood from the back door to the beach.

"The couple's only daughter said the last time she saw her parents alive was Saturday night around nine when they left her home in Wakoola Springs after having dinner. She said nothing seemed amiss at the time.

"Investigators said, at the rear of the home, they found footsteps in the sand from the back door to the beach, which indicated a struggle had occurred between the couple and their abductors.

"From all indications, investigators said, the couple was abducted, then taken out to sea. Over the past three days, search teams have been dragging the ocean floor behind the house, but, thus far, have found nothing."

Bobby looked up from the newspaper. Now the whole world knew about the deed he and Lucky had committed. If discovered, they would be vilified and reviled until the end of time. He trembled at the thought.

***

That night, Bobby had a dream. He dreamed that Lucky had thrown Miss Margaret into the water, then he had jumped in and saved her. Back in the boat, Bobby and Lucky fought and Bobby managed to take the gun away from Lucky and kill him. As the boat pulled back into the marina, people were on the docks hailing and applauding him. Suddenly, he awoke from the dream. He rubbed his eyes, then looked around. Reality had set in again. He burst into laughter. His laughter was so loud, Idella woke up.

"Bobby, what's so funny!!"

"Nothing," he said. "Go back to sleep."

Seeking Peace

The following morning when he awoke, he wanted to see Lazarus. He liked and trusted Lazarus. The teenager didn't judge or criticize or ask questions. Bobby knew Lazarus would not be out of school until mid-afternoon. He didn't want to fish. He just wanted to talk. Lazarus didn't have an agenda and would give him heartfelt, honest answers.

Just after two, Bobby saw Lazarus getting off the school bus. Then he watched as the teenager, lugging several books, started toward the forest of sea oats to his home.

"Lazarus!" Bobby called.

The teenager turned.

"Hey, Bobby," he said. "What you doing?"

"Want to go for a walk on the beach?"

"Sure," he replied. "Let me put up my books. I'll meet you at the cove."

Ten minutes later, Bobby and Lazarus, pants legs rolled up and barefooted, were strolling down the beach, wading in the tidal pools. Bobby started the conversation innocently.

"How's school going?" he asked.

"Oh, fine," the teenager replied.

They walked quietly. The tide was going out and the sharp undertow was sloshing huge globs of wet sand about their feet and ankles.

"Lazarus," Bobby started. "What do you think God is?"

"God?" the teenager asked, looking at him quizzically. "Come on, Bobby. You know what God is. Everybody knows that God created all of this," he said with a sweep of his hand. "All the land and sky and water and animals and birds. It says that in the Bible."

"He's going to have to be one big guy."

"He is!" Lazarus says. "My grandmother says God is everything."

"Do you really believe that," Bobby asked. "Way down deep in your heart?"

"I sure do," Lazarus said. "I believe in Jesus because I believe in Grandma. Grandma says one of these days the clouds are going to open up and Jesus Christ in all his glory will walk across the sky and stand in judgment before all human beings."

Bobby didn't answer at first.

"When you think of Jesus, does it give peace in your heart?"

"Sure does," Lazarus said. "I can feel all of me when I'm with Jesus."

Bobby studied him for a moment.

"What do you think happens to you when you die?" he asked.

"Well," Lazarus began thoughtfully, "if you've been a good person on this earth, you'll go to heaven and spend your days in peace and harmony with God while he sits on his golden throne..."

"What if you've been a bad person?" Bobby asked.

"Then you go to hell and burn in a fire that is hotter than a million suns," Lazarus said.

Lazarus looked at Bobby to determine if his answer was satisfactory.

"You know all of this," he said. "You go to church. You've read the Bible."

Bobby was quiet for several minutes.

"You ever done anything bad?" Bobby asked.

"Well, sometimes I take a nickel from Grandma's change purse so I can buy an ice cream at school," he said. "I think Grandma knows I'm doing it, but she don't say nothing."

Bobby laughed.

"That's the worst thing you ever done?"

"Yep," Lazarus said. "That's the worst."

Bobby was quiet again.

"Are you afraid to die, Bobby?" Lazarus asked.

Bobby paused before he answered.

"Not really afraid," Bobby said. "When I was in Korea, I faced death every day and wasn't afraid. I just wondered what it would be like after I was gone..."

"Is there something worrying you?" Lazarus asked.

"No, why do you ask?"

"You seem like you're all balled up inside," he said. "You seem like you're looking for something and can't find it."

Bobby didn't answer.

"What you looking for?" Lazarus asked.

"Nothing really," Bobby lied with a nervous laugh. "I don't know why you think that."

"Why you asking me all these questions?" Lazarus asked.

"I was just wondering how you felt about these things," he said. "Ready to head back?"

"Yeah," Lazarus replied. "If you are..."

As they turned and started walking back down the beach, Bobby knew he needed help. Until now, he had always been absolutely certain of his mental stability. In fact, there had never been a question. Now, after what he had done, he wasn't so sure anymore. He needed something beyond himself. Something solid he could hold on to. At the moment, he was feeling very, very fragile. Maybe Lazarus was right. Maybe there was something in the church and religion he wasn't seeing. Maybe there really was some old man with a staff out there somewhere in the galaxies that pulled all the strings. Maybe he should investigate further.

***

The following morning, en route to work, all that Train and Clifford talked about was the murders.

"There were tracks in the sand from the back of the house to the beach," Train said. "The police believe whoever took them out of the house dumped them in the ocean. Probably took 'em out to the Gulf Stream. You get dumped in that Gulf Stream, you're gone."

"Why would somebody want to do something like that?" Clifford asked. "To a judge…"

"Somebody wanted revenge for some sentence he passed," Train said. "That's usually why judges get killed. Somebody gets a long sentence in prison, then when they get out, they kill the judge that gave it."

Bobby walked, listening but not speaking.

***

On Saturday night, Bobby was back at the beach sipping shine, trying to analyze his dilemma. He searched through his mind, trying to discover some reason why this entire experience had been visited upon him. Of all the people that Lucky could have picked to bring on the boat this night, why did one of them have to be Miss Margaret? His thoughts wandered back to Kim Song Park, a Korean woman he had known during his years in Korea. She said everything that happened in life was the result of karma. Any bad thing you do, she said, you will pay for it sooner or later. You harvest what you plant, she said. He wondered if there was something he did in the past that had brought this upon him.

Once when he was eleven years old, a white woman in Wakoola Springs asked him to help her get rid of some stray cats. She had been a friend of Calvin's and, during the summers, Calvin would do odd jobs for her. Cut her grass. Rake her yard and such. Then one summer when Calvin went to visit his uncle, she asked Bobby to help her get rid of the cats who had overrun an abandoned house she owned. She promised to pay Bobby fifty cents for each cat he removed. When Bobby asked how she wanted to get rid of them, she said to do anything he liked. So the following day, Bobby caught nine of the cats, placed them in an old onion sack, and dumped them in a canal near the inlet. As the onion sack slowly sank into the water, the cats were meowing pitifully as they met their deaths. Even several days later, Bobby could still hear their pitiful cries in his mind. After he drowned the cats, he didn't go back to collect the $4.50. In fact, he hated himself for what he had done. He hated himself for allowing himself to be talked into doing such a thing. Did the fact that he drowned the cats result in his committing the terrible crime visited upon Miss Margaret and her husband? Had karma come back to avenge the deaths of the cats?

***

The following Sunday, Bobby decided to go to church. He had not attended services in three weeks. Down deep inside, he was seeking some sort of salvation wherever he thought he could find it. Rev. Jenkins was preaching on the book of Revelation. He read from the Bible as he strode in front of the pulpit.

"Then another sign appeared in heaven: an enormous red dragon with seven heads and ten horns and seven crowns on its heads. Its tail swept a third of the stars out of the sky and flung them to the earth. The dragon stood in front of the woman who was about to give birth, so that it might devour her child the moment he was born…"

Bobby wondered what he would do if he saw a red dragon with a tail so large it swept the stars out of the sky. He found peace in the words, but his credibility to believe them was sorely lacking. After church services, as Bobby and Idella walked back along Sand River Road, Bobby felt calmer within himself. He wasn't sure how or why, but the services had brought a new solace to his spirit. He welcomed that so much.

***

On Monday morning, Bobby, Clifford, and Train were walking down Sand River Road to work. As they neared the church, Bobby told them to go ahead of him.

"Where you going?" Train asked.

Bobby didn't answer. Quickly, he strode across the church parking lot to the front door and tried to open it. It was locked. He walked around to the side and tried to raise a window. It was also locked. Bobby shaded his eyes against the sun and tried to peek inside. Inside, it was dark and empty. Bobby turned and started back to the road.

"You got religion these days?" Clifford asked.

Bobby didn't answer.

"Man, you know you really been acting strange lately," Train said.

Little White Church

The following morning, Bobby was up early. Once he had breakfast and fresh overalls, he was walking down Sand River Road to the church. As he approached, he could see Howard, the church janitor, raking leaves at the side of the church. Bobby greeted the janitor, then strode across the churchyard to the front door.

Once he was in front of the door, he shook it. It was still locked.

"The church ain't open today," Howard said.

"What if I need to pray?" Bobby said.

"You'll just have to wait."

"I can't pray outside of church," Bobby said.

The old man shook his head.

"You just have to wait until Friday night for prayer services," Howard said.

Bobby turned and went to the side of the church. He tried to raise a window. It was locked. Bobby started checking the other windows.

"Bobby, what you doing?" Howard asked. "You can't go in the church when it's locked up."

"You can't let me in for a few minutes?"

"No," Howard said. "Rev. Jenkins would be mad. I could lose my job."

"It can't hurt anything," Bobby said.

Suddenly, he found an unlocked window. He opened it.

"Bobby, don't do that!"

Bobby didn't hear. Seconds later, he slipped through the open window and into the church.

Inside the church, columns of morning light streamed through the windows on either side. Bobby looked around at the pulpit and the huge white cross behind it. He didn't know where to start. He had never tried to pray before. He had seen others do it, but he had never tried it himself. He knelt down in front of the altar and closed his eyes. This was how he had seen others do it.

"Oh Lord," he began. "I've put myself in a hole that I can't get out of. I'm afraid my soul has been lost for all time. Please help me. Tell me what I can do to get away from this terrible pain. I can't see my way out of it. I need help and I feel like you can help me."

He stopped and opened his eyes. He looked around at the pews, the cross, and the pulpit. Somehow, he felt silly. Who was he talking to, he asked himself. To these concrete walls? To the white cross? Was praying just talking to yourself?

Suddenly, he heard a loud knocking sound on the church door.

He wondered who it could be. Bobby stood up and started for the church door. Suddenly, the door opened. At first, in the bright light streaming through the open door into the darkened church, all he saw was a silhouette of a large man. Then, as the image clarified itself, a huge electric shock shot through his body when he recognized Sheriff Cunningham. Upon recognition, he froze inside. Then his legs went wobbly and he fainted dead away on the church floor.

Several seconds later, he awoke. Sheriff Cunningham was bending over him.

"Bobby! Bobby!!" the sheriff was saying. "What's wrong with you?"

"I didn't do it! I didn't do it!" Bobby blurted out helplessly.

"Didn't do what?" the sheriff asked. "What you talking about?"

As he slowly regained consciousness, Bobby knew he had to think of an explanation.

"Oh, Sheriff Cunningham," he said, finally gaining full consciousness again. "I'm glad to see you."

"What's wrong?" the sheriff asked again.

"I haven't been feeling well lately," he said. "I needed to come in the church for a few minutes."

"You can't go in the church if it's not open," the sheriff said.

"Well, this was sort of an emergency," Bobby said.

The sheriff inhaled. He had the situation under control now.

"Okay, come on!" he said.

The sheriff reached down, gave Bobby his hand, and pulled him to his feet. The sheriff could feel Bobby's hand trembling.

For a moment, the sheriff peered at him.

"Why are you so nervous?" the sheriff asked.

"I hadn't been sleeping well lately," Bobby said.

"You feeling better now?" the sheriff asked.

"Oh, yeah," Bobby replied. "Much better."

"Then go on home and get some sleep," he said. "You ain't done no harm here. Howard called me because he was afraid he would lose his job."

"That's okay, sheriff," Bobby said. "I understand."

***

On Wednesday, the following day, Bobby put in another day at the sugar mill. He had slept little the previous night and as he walked, he could barely keep his eyes open. At the roller controls, he fell asleep twice. The second time, he suddenly awoke when the rollers started making a thumping noise. This meant there were too many cane stalks in the hopper.

"Shut her down!" Carl ordered.

Bobby switched off the engine, then he and the foreman crawled into the mouth of the hopper and started manually removing the stalks that had jammed the rollers. After some thirty minutes, Carl ordered Bobby to start the engine again. The machine was operating properly now. They had lost forty minutes of work, but the foreman didn't say anything. Finally, when the day ended, it was all Bobby could do to make it home. As Bobby, Train, and Clifford walked down Sand River Road, Bobby said nothing the entire route.

"There's something bad wrong going on with you, Bobby," Clifford said as he veered off toward his home. "If there is anything I can do to help, let me know."

Bobby didn't answer.

Some twenty minutes later, when Bobby reached his home, Idella was waiting.

"Hey, baby," she said. "How was work today?"

Bobby looked at her, said nothing, then brushed past her into the house.

"Oh, Lord," she said. "Here we go again."

Inside, in the bedroom, she watched as he removed his clothes and crawled into bed.

"All you want to do lately is sleep," she said. "What's going on?"

"Get away from me," he said. "Leave me alone."

Idella shook her head in frustration, then turned and slammed the bedroom door.

***

On Friday, when Bobby woke up, he knew he couldn't go to work. He didn't care anymore. He stayed in bed all day. That afternoon, he awoke to see his mother standing over him.

"Mama," he said. "What are you doing here?"

"I come to see about my baby," she said. "I brought the doctor."

"Doctor?" Bobby said. "I don't need no doctor."

Behind his mother, he could see Dr. McDermott, the white doctor from Wakoola Springs who had been their family physician for many years.

"Now he's going to take a look at you whether you want him to or not," his mother said. "You need some help!"

"Oh, Mama!" Bobby said. "Okay. Go ahead."

Over the next thirty minutes, the doctor checked his vital signs, then Bobby removed his shirt while the doctor checked his chest and heart. Finally, having finished, the doctor motioned for Hattie to step outside with him.

"He's not sleeping," the doctor said. "His blood pressure is up and his heart rate is abnormally high. There is something on his mind."

"What is it?" the mother asked.

"I don't know that," the doctor said. "And I don't think he's going to tell us. I can give him some sleeping pills," he replied. "Maybe that will help."

***

Bobby spent all day Thursday at the beach sipping shine. He wanted to slip away from the world and all of humankind. He didn't care about anything anymore. All of the reasons he had for living were now gone. He felt there was nothing left.

On Friday morning, he was still asleep at 8 a.m.

When he awoke, Idella was standing over him.

"Bobby," she asked. "You going to work today?"

He sat up, rubbed his eyes, and looked at her.

"You going to work today?" she asked again.

"Work?" He laughed. "Who needs to work?"

"You do have to buy food and pay the rent," she said.

Bobby laughed. "Leave me alone," he said. "Just go away and leave me alone."

Singing at the Beach

That night, bottle in hand, Bobby was strolling along the beach. As he looked across the great expanse of water and sky, he felt a unity with something outside of himself. He felt at one with the ocean and the sky. The feeling of unity, the sense of belonging to something beyond himself, brought a much-needed peace. Suddenly, he started to sing.

"On Jordan's stormy banks I stand and cast a wistful eye to Canaan's fair and happy land where my procession lies. I am bound for the promised laaand, I am bound for the promised land, Oh who will come and go with me, I am bound for the promised land."

He stopped. Now the only sound was the wind and the grating roar of the waves crashing on the beach. Suddenly, he heard a voice.

Startled, he turned.

In the moonlight, he could make out the diminutive figure of Idella.

"Bobby!! Bobby Lincoln!" she said. "What on God's earth are you doing?"

"I'm singing," he said. "What's wrong with that?"

"I been wondering what you were doing down here every night. You down here singing church songs?"

"Looks that way," he said.

Idella inhaled and shook her head.

"Something bad has happened to you," she said. "You ain't the Bobby Lincoln I've been knowing all these years."

"Well, then go back to the house and mind your own business."

"As long as I live under the same roof as you, your business is my business."

He didn't answer. He started to sing again.

"I'm on the rock at last, at last, I'm on the rock at last, my feet have found a resting place, I'm on the rock at last."

"Bobby, what's wrong with you?" she pleaded. "It's like you're going crazy or something."

"Go on and leave me alone," he said.

In the bright moonlight, he could see her peering at him.

"Oh, Bobby! Bobby, baby!" she said. "I'm going crazy seeing you like this."

Suddenly, she rushed to him and threw herself in his arms. She held tightly to his waist, then she peered up into his face.

"Please tell me what's wrong?" she pleaded. "I love you!! I love you!! Don't you know that? Don't that mean anything to you?"

She buried her face in his chest and started sobbing.

"Bobby," she said between the sobs. "I love you. I want to help you. Don't you know that?"

He pushed her away.

"Don't push me away," she said. "Talk to me!!"

In the moonlight, she could see his dour, expressionless face.

"Leave me alone," he said. "Just go away."

Suddenly, she broke the embrace. Then she turned from him, screaming and crying, and ran back toward the house. As he watched her disappear into the mangrove and palmetto undergrowth, it crossed Bobby's mind that he had no interest in Idella any longer. He was preoccupied with the monster in his mind.

Moments later, he was singing again.

***

The following afternoon, Bobby had a visit from Clifford. Bobby was sitting on the back porch.

"I got a message for you from the foreman," Clifford said.

"What's that?"

"Carl said to tell you, if you ain't back at work on Monday, he's going to get somebody else to run the rollers."

Bobby peered at Clifford.

"He said you were asleep on the job and ruined a batch of cane on Monday. He's not happy with you."

Bobby laughed.

"A job? Who needs a job?"

Clifford peered at him.

"Tell him to go ahead and fire me," Bobby continued. "I don't give a damn."

"You going to give up your job?" Clifford asked. "Just like that?"

Bobby laughed.

"Yeah," he said. "Just like that!"

"He's going to fire you, Bobby," Clifford said. "I'm telling you. You ain't going to have a job."

"You tell that old white man to stick it where the sun don't shine," Bobby said.

Clifford shook his head in frustration, then turned and walked out the door.

Visit with Lucky

The next morning, Bobby was up early. Somehow, when he woke that morning, he felt like he needed to talk to Lucky. He wanted to see if the deed they committed was having the same effects on the big Brazilian. When he arrived at the marina, he went into the restaurant first, but Lucky was nowhere in sight. When he ventured down the dock to *Lucky's Lady*, there was a closed sign on the gangway. The sign instructed charter customers to call a phone number. In the adjacent boat slip, Bobby saw David Morris, the owner of a shrimp boat, whom he knew.

"Where's Lucky?" Bobby asked.

"He's gone to Titusville," the fisherman replied. "He's got a wife up there."

"Okay," Bobby said. "I've heard about her."

"He'll be back around noon."

***

That afternoon, Bobby was back. As he neared *Lucky's Lady*, he saw Lucky sitting on deck, drinking a beer and smoking a cigarette.

"Bobby," he said. "Come aboard!"

Bobby walked down the gangplank and had a seat in a deck chair.

"How you been doing?" Lucky asked.

"Not so good," Bobby replied. "Been having lots of bad feelings about what we did."

Somehow, it was an enormous relief to have somebody to be able to talk to about it.

"Well," Lucky said. "It's history now. Nobody can change what's already been done."

"You don't have any bad feelings about what we did?"

"Maybe," he said. "A little, but I just don't think about it."

"I'm in misery about what we did to that old couple," Bobby said. "It has ruined my life."

"Bobby," Lucky said. "We committed the perfect crime. No bodies. No witnesses. No evidence. No charges. It's that simple. As long as we keep our mouths shut, nobody will ever suspect us."

"For me, there is more to it than that."

"What else is there?"

"I have to live with myself," Bobby said. "I been knowing that woman since I was a child and she had always been good to me."

"If you got a guilty conscience, that's your fault," Lucky said. "A guilty conscience is for losers. I like winning myself."

"Don't you have a conscience?"

"Sure I have a conscience," Lucky said, "but I also have a sense of self-preservation. I can block things out of my head."

"I can't," Bobby said. "I don't know how to do that."

Lucky didn't answer.

"Has anybody talked to you?" Bobby asked.

"Who's there to talk to?" Lucky said "The police were down here yesterday talking to Carmelo. They were asking questions about anyone who might have taken a boat from the marina that Saturday night, but they didn't get anything."

Long pause.

"You don't have bad dreams about what we did?"

Lucky laughed.

"Maybe a little," he said. "Í just don't think about it."

"How do you do that?"

"I just blot it out of my mind."

"I don't know how to do that," Bobby said. "I keep seeing the face of that woman as she went down into the water."

Lucky studied Bobby for a long moment.

"You don't remember that old woman's face?" Bobby asked.

"Yeah," Lucky said calmly. "I remember."

"That doesn't bother you?"

Lucky laughed.

Maybe a little," he said. "I just don't think about it."

"Well, I do," Bobby said.

Lucky took a deep breath and shook his head.

"If you keep going on like this, you're going to get both of us in a lot of trouble," he said. "What we did has got to remain a secret. If word gets out..."

He didn't finish.

"Bobby," he said. "You've got to get over this."

"I wish I could," Bobby said.

"You're letting your conscience get the better of you," Lucky said. "That's dangerous. You never know where it will lead."

Bobby didn't answer.

"Now if you start feeling sorry for yourself and go to the law with this," Lucky said, "I'll hunt you down and put you out of your misery."

Bobby laughed.

"You and whose army?" Bobby replied.

Bobby stood up from the deck chair.

"Where you going?"

"I'm going downstairs, get a couple pints of shine, and I'm going home."

"Remember what I told you," Lucky said.

Bobby didn't reply, then started down the gangway.

Lucky quickly stepped forward and grabbed Bobby's shirt.

"Don't walk away from me when I'm talking to you," Lucky said. Bobby could see the anger in his eyes. "If you tell anybody what we did," Lucky said, still holding Bobby's shirt. "I'll see you are put in your grave."

"Get your God-damn hands off me," Bobby said, slapping Lucky's hand away.

Bobby turned and started walking down the gangway. Lucky glared after him in livid anger.

Bobby didn't look back.

***

That afternoon, when Bobby returned home, he saw a car, its engine running, waiting out front. Inside, he found Idella. She was dressed up and had a suitcase in her hand.

"Who is that out there?" he asked.

"That's my Uncle Robert," she said. "He's going to take me to Manatee. I'm leaving, Bobby."

"Go ahead," he said. "You don't need to be around me when I'm like this…"

"Bobby, why won't you tell me what's happened to you?"

Bobby shook his head.

"Just go on," he said. "After all this is over, maybe you and me can have a life together. Till then, you'll be better off without me."

"Why don't you have time for me anymore?" she asked. "If we're going to be together, we have to share our lives together. Why can't you tell me what's going on?"

"Don't start now," he said. "Just go away."

"I've loved you and tried to be as good to you as I know how. Lately, I don't know who you are."

Bobby shook his head in disgust.

"There's no hope for you," she said. "I've loved you and believed in you and tried to do the best I can, but now I can see there is no hope. You don't care about nothing any more..."

"Save your breath," he said with a wave of his hand. "Go on!! I've got other things to worry about."

Idella didn't like being dismissed.

Angrily, she turned to him.

"I know you are young and think you know everything and don't need nobody. The day will come, Bobby Lincoln," she said, shaking her finger, "when you will get down on your knees and beg me to come back to you."

He laughed.

"That will never happen," he said. "Not in a million years."

"You need help, Bobby," she said. "You need to go to some mental hospital or somewhere like that so they can help you."

"Talk! Talk! Talk!" he said.

She stopped. She could see she was getting nowhere.

"Is that all?" he asked.

"That's all," she said.

Then she turned quickly, picked up the suitcase, and went out the door. After the door closed, Bobby went to the window and watched as the car pulled out of the yard and headed down Sand River Road. His eyes glistened with tears as the car disappeared into the distance.

Baptism

With the departure of Idella, Bobby's sanity was near its end. The deed he had done had cost him everything in his life he had taken for granted. His job, his peace of mind, Idella, and now his very sanity was in question. That night, Bobby went to the beach with a bottle. For more than two hours, he walked along the beach singing gospel hymns and listening to the grating roar of the incoming tide. In the distance, he could see a rain coming into shore.

The great monster that had taken up residence in his soul had become larger than he was. The only peace he could find was in the moonshine. He had to have some relief from somewhere. His mind wandered back to Rev. Jenkins and his offer of baptism. Maybe baptism would quell the storm in his mind and allow him to sleep at night. Many times, he had attended baptisms with his mother. Time after time, he had watched as those whose souls had been cleansed came out of the water praising the lord as if they were new, reborn people. In particular, he remembered Carlotta Williams. Bobby had known Carlotta when he was a student at Carver High. She was three years older than Bobby, but they were still good friends. In high school, everybody knew she was a loose woman. Then when she graduated, she went to work at Stella's, a house of prostitution in Blue Springs. One day, to Bobby's surprise, she appeared as a baptismal candidate at the church. Bobby remembered that the minute she came out of the water, she was filled with happiness and praising the Lord. Two weeks later, she got married, moved to Wakoola Springs, and started raising a family. The last time Bobby had seen her, she was working at the five and dime in Wakoola Springs. He wondered if baptism could do that for him. At least it was a hope.

***

Three days later, after his mother had a word with Rev. Jenkins, Bobby was about to discover the effects baptism would have on him. On this particular Sunday, some forty parishioners from Ebenezer Church had gathered on the banks of Tomoka Creek to witness the baptism of Bobby and three others. The edges of the baptismal area had been blocked off with wire mesh to prevent alligators from trespassing. A year earlier, a thirteen-year-old girl who was being baptized had been attacked and eaten by an alligator. As parishioners watched in horror, the alligator wrested the poor girl from the arms of the minister, then carried her out to deeper water. She was never seen again.

As the ceremony began, one by one, Rev. Jenkins, decked out in his dark blue baptismal robe, met each of the candidates at the creek's bank, then escorted them into the waist-deep water. When each of the first three emerged dripping wet from the cold creek water, they were praising Jesus. Then it came Bobby's turn.

As with the others, Rev. Jenkins met him at the water's edge, then took his arm and led him into waist-deep water. Finally, they stopped.

The preacher and Bobby bowed their heads in prayer.

"Oh Heavenly Father," Rev. Jenkins said, looking skyward, "we come to you as your humble servant today asking you to bless and cleanse this poor sinner of the evil which the world has set upon him. We know there is no escape from the evil of this world and we turn to your great power and wisdom to heal the evils which the world has wrought upon this poor sinner so that he may live again in the divine light of your power and love. This I pray in your glorious name. Amen."

Then he turned to Bobby and placed his hand over Bobby's mouth and nose.

"I now baptize you in the name of the Father, the Son, and the Holy Ghost."

He laid Bobby back into the cold water for a brief moment, then raised him to a standing position again.

On shore, the other parishioners shouted, "Amen!!"

Seconds later, Bobby was back on shore, then went into a privacy tent where he could dry off and change clothes. During the ride back to Palm Harbor in the preacher's car, Bobby waited for the new cleansed person to step forward. He didn't feel any different. There was no redeeming glow inside his heart. He was the same Bobby Lincoln he had been the day before. *Maybe it takes a while*, Bobby thought, and he should wait. That night, he did manage to sleep. He had a calmness he hadn't felt the day before. The next morning, however, the great monster that he knew so well once again became the primary preoccupation of his mind. By now, he knew only too well its debilitating effects on him and the dominance it waged over his mind. The grace of God had not found Bobby.

Now he was back at square one. His head hurt with every thought. Thinking was a disease. All day, Bobby lay in the bed in a semi-comatose state. His mind was reeling in and out. He wanted to stay in bed. He didn't want to be part of the real world any longer. It was too painful.

He stayed drunk all of the following day. When he awoke the following afternoon, the sun was going down and he was hungry. He hadn't eaten in two days. Outside, he went to the chicken coop and took four eggs. Then, one at a time, he punched a hole in the end of the egg and sucked out the insides. Then he looked around at his world. The backyard, the shed, the house, and Sand River Road. None of it had any meaning now. *This is the end*, he thought. *Now I've lost everything. You ain't got nothing left,* he told himself.

That night, Bobby was back at the beach. With a bottle in one hand, he walked from "Sea Oats Cove" to the jetty at the inlet. There he sat on the rocks and watched the incoming tide crash across the rocks. For almost an hour, he sat sipping shine and listening to the tide. Finally, he started back down the beach to his home. As he walked, he suddenly noticed a small, dark figure moving slowly up the beach toward him. *Who could that be?* he thought. No one lived around here within a quarter of a mile. Why would someone be strolling on the beach at this hour? As the figure drew closer, Bobby could see it looked like a woman.

Yes, it was a woman. She appeared frail and bent over. As Bobby drew nearer, he thought it might be Idella. But then he knew she was in Manatee. Then, seconds later, he recognized the face and drew back in horror. It was Miss Margaret and, on her face, she had the same pitiful look she had the night he and Lucky had dropped her over the side of the boat. Now Bobby could see that the load she was carrying was diving weights. Suddenly, he screamed, then broke into a dead run back up the beach to his home. Finally, reaching the back porch, he stopped, breathless and terrified. He was sweating, his heart was racing, and he was trembling. *Miss Margaret has come back for me*, he thought. *She has returned to exact her vengeance.* Suddenly, in an act of pure fear, he darted into the house and climbed into bed.

***

Back in the house, he went into the bedroom and peered in the mirror. He didn't know the person who was staring back at him. He looked tired and depressed. His eyes were bleary from lack of sleep. He was unwashed, unshaven, and he could smell the odor coming from his body. *What the holy hell happened to you, nigga?* he asked himself. Over the next hour, he drank another pint of moonshine and then lay down in bed.

Finally, he drifted off to sleep and started to dream. In the dream, he saw a crowd of people gathered at a gallows. Then, as his eyes searched through the crowd, he drew back in horror when he saw his mother. Who did his mother know that was being hung? Then he peered at the condemned man. When he saw the man's face, terror filled his soul. The condemned man was him. He screamed and was suddenly wide awake. He reached under the bed for a bottle, then sat on the edge of the bed. Outside, he could hear the wind howling. He took a drink and lay back down. For a moment, he dozed off, then he heard a knock on the door.

He wondered who could be visiting this time of night.

Bobby got out of bed and opened the door. No one was there. He stepped out on the porch and looked around. There was no one, only a misting rain and the sound of the wind whipping in from the ocean.

He returned inside to the bed.

Moments later, he heard knocking on the door again.

Again, he got up and went to the door. Again, there was no one, only the wind howling in the night.

I'm losing my mind, he thought. *It is finally really happening.*

Once again, he returned to bed and dozed off again.

Ten minutes later, he woke up to the sound of someone calling his name.

"Bobby! Bobby!" the voice called.

That's not a real voice, Bobby told himself. *Like the knock on the door, that's just a sound in my head.*

Again, he dozed off to sleep, then moments later, he heard knocking on the bedroom window.

"Bobby! Bobby!" a voice was calling.

Then there was a sharp rapping at the bedroom window.

"Bobby! Bobby!"

Suddenly, he recognized his mother's voice.

He went to the window and opened it.

Outside, Bobby saw his mother and Clifford standing in a drizzling rain.

"Mama! What you doing here?"

"Open the door," she said. "We're getting wet out here."

Mother's Love

Moments later, Bobby's mother and Clifford were inside the house. His mother looked around. The house was a shambles. The sink was piled high with dishes. Flies were swarming over rotting food on the counter. Clothes and pieces of trash were scattered about the floor. The trashcan had turned over and old coffee grounds and leftover food had spilled out and was rotting on the floor.

Bobby's mother shook her head in disgust.

"Oh great God, baby," she said. "What have you done to yourself?"

Bobby didn't reply.

The mother turned to inspect him.

"Look at you!" she said. "You hadn't shaved, you hadn't bathed, you haven't been eating right. All you been doing is drinking this devil's brew."

She kicked an empty shine bottle on the floor.

Bobby didn't look at her.

"I want you to come stay at my house for a while," she said. "I'll take care of you until you're better."

"I'm telling you, Mama," he said, "I'm fine."

Unsteadily, he stood up from the chair to prove his point. For a moment, he remained upright, then collapsed on the floor.

His mother shook her head in frustration.

"See what I mean?" she said.

"Come on, Bobby," Clifford said. "Let me help you up."

Clifford reached down his hand, Bobby took it, and his old friend pulled him to his feet.

"Come on," Clifford said. "Let's go to your mother's house."

***

Over the next thirty minutes, the three made their way down Sand River Road to Bobby's mother's house. Upon arrival, she put Bobby in bed and instructed him to sleep as long as he liked.

"Now you ain't having none of that devil's brew in my house," she said.

Bobby didn't reply.

That day he spent at his mother's home. After he slept away most of the day, he got up and his mother made him shave, bathe, and put on fresh clothes. She fed him bean soup and cornbread, then he went back to bed. Late that night, he awoke.

"Mama!" he called.

"I'm in here, baby," she said, calling from the living room.

Bobby got up and went into the living room. His mother was seated in a rocking chair, reading the Bible.

"How you feeling, baby?" she asked.

"A lot better," he said.

"Want me to make you a cup of tea?"

"Please," he said.

Moments later, she sat a cup of hot, steaming tea in front of him, then took her seat again to read the Bible.

For several minutes, they sat quietly, Bobby sipping tea and his mother reading the Bible.

Then suddenly, Bobby blurted out the words, "Mama, I can't do it anymore."

She looked up from her Bible.

"What you talking 'bout?" she asked. "Can't do what anymore?"

"I can't run anymore," he said.

"Run from what?"

"Oh, Mama!" he said, bursting into tears, "I've done a terrible thing."

"What you done?"

Bobby stood, then collapsed on the floor. Then he started crawling on his hands and knees across the floor to his mother.

"Oh baby, my baby!!" she said. "Oh great God, what have you done?"

Upon reaching his mother, still on his knees, he buried his face in her lap like a little child. His mother placed her hands over his head protectively.

"I helped kill 'em, Mama," he said.

"What you talking about?" she asked. "Helped kill who?"

"The Chillingsworths!" he said. Then he buried his face in his mother's lap and began sobbing.

"Oh great God," she said, placing the side of her head atop her son's head. "What devil got into yo head that made you do something like that?"

"I don't know what happened, Mama," he said. "I just went crazy for a few minutes."

The mother raised her head and peered skyward.

"Oh God," she said. "What did I ever do to have you visit something like this on me and my son?"

Then, weeping softly, she placed her head on her son's head again.

"Oh, baby," she said. "When I pushed you out my womb, I loved you. Now that I might live to see you go to your grave, I still love you."

Then, suddenly, she felt a call to action. She raised her head, then lifted her son's head out of her lap.

"I'm going to go across the street and talk to the reverend," she said. "I'm going to have him call the law."

"Oh, Mama," he said. "I'm sorry. I'm so sorry for what I did."

"Oh, baby," she said. "There's not much we can do about it now."

***

Thirty minutes later, Rev. Jenkins and Bobby's mother answered a knock on the door. It was Sheriff Cunningham.

"Come on in, sheriff," the mother said.

Together, the three went into the living room, where they found Bobby seated on the couch.

"Bobby has something to tell you," the mother said.

The sheriff peered at Bobby.

"What you want to tell me, Bobby?"

"I helped kill the Chillingsworths," he said.

The sheriff didn't react.

"I should have suspected something like this after what happened that day in the church," the sheriff said. "You've got to go with me, Bobby. I'm taking you to jail."

Jail

Twenty minutes later, Bobby and the sheriff were riding quietly along Sand River Road in a county squad car. Finally, the sheriff spoke. Bobby could hear the quiet anger in this voice.

"Bobby, I can't believe you would get involved in something like this," he said. "What got into you?"

"I don't know, sheriff," he said. "I guess I messed up pretty good, didn't I?"

"It couldn't be much worse," the sheriff said. "My God, Bobby. Yo daddy would turn over in his grave if he knew you were involved in something like this."

Bobby didn't answer.

"What got into you?" the sheriff asked again.

Bobby didn't reply.

"I guess it's too late to do anything now," the sheriff said. "It's going to break yo mama's heart."

Bobby didn't reply.

***

The Wakoola County Courthouse was a whitewashed stucco structure that stood five blocks due west of Old Dixie Highway in the heart of Wakoola Springs. Surrounded on all sides by melaleuca trees, the courthouse, at four stories, was the tallest building in Wakoola County and could be seen up to five miles away in any direction. To the south, adjacent to the courthouse, stood the county jail. Between the two structures, a sheltered walkway had been built along which prisoners were taken to and from jail.

Fifteen minutes later, Sheriff Cunningham was escorting Bobby along the walkway. In the booking room, a sleepy-eyed, middle-aged white man made a mug shot and fingerprinted Bobby, then gave him a striped jail uniform and a pair of sandals. Finally, with chained hands and feet, Bobby was led up the stairs to the cellblock on the fourth floor. The jail was a dingy affair. The smell of urine hung in the air, the lighting was poor, and, as the cellblock door clanged shut behind him, Bobby saw a rat skitter across the floor.

"No. 3," the deputy said.

Bobby stopped in front of the designated cell. The deputy unlocked the door.

"Go on!" he said.

Bobby shuffled inside and the deputy removed the chains.

"Breakfast at seven," the deputy said. "If you ain't up to get your food, you don't get none."

Then he turned and, seconds later, Bobby heard the steel door clang shut behind him.

Bobby looked around. The cell was an eight-by-ten rectangle with steel walls on either side, a sink and a toilet, and a barred window at the rear with heavy mesh wire on the outside. The bunkbed was made of steel springs and a thin mattress. It was cold. Bobby grabbed a blanket off the top bunk, removed his clothes to his shorts, and crawled under the blanket. The only light was in the hallway and Bobby peered down at the shadow of the bars on the cell floor. *I guess you've done it now*, he told himself. *This will be your home for the rest of your life.* Somehow, now that he had confessed, the nagging monster of the past three weeks was gone. By telling someone, by revealing the terrible secret he had been hiding, he felt immeasurably better about himself. At least he wasn't running anymore. He wasn't fleeing the great monster that had been burrowing into his very soul since the murders. Maybe he could sleep now. And he did. It was the first night of sound rest he had had in over three weeks.

***

The following morning, Bobby was awakened by the sound of the Florida East Coast train, which roared past promptly at seven a.m. Bobby raised himself on one elbow and rubbed his eyes. Voices filled the air. In the cell across the corridor, he saw two other inmates, a tall, thin teenager and a sullen, older, middle-aged man. Seeing Bobby was awake, the younger one called to him.

"Hey, man!!"

Bobby looked over.

"I'm Darnell and this is Tyrone," he said. "What's yo name?"

"Bobby!"

"What you in for?"

"Capital murder," Bobby said. "The murder of Judge Chillingsworth and his wife."

Darnell eyes grew as big as saucers.

"Holy Christ!" he said. "You killed the judge?"

Bobby nodded.

"Man, I wouldn't want to be in yo shoes," Darnell said, shaking his head in amazement. "They got me for armed robbery – but murdering a judge. Man, oh man! You gotta be one bad nigger. I ain't getting nowhere near you."

The older man turned to the teenager.

"Shut up, you little punk!!" he said. "You don't know nothing!"

"Yes, sir!!" Darnell replied.

Tyrone turned to Bobby. "You got a lawyer?" he asked. "I mean, a real lawyer?"

"No," Bobby said. "Got a public defender."

"Then you ain't got a chance," Tyrone said. "You as good as in the electric chair."

"Maybe so," Bobby said. "But I ain't afraid."

Tyrone peered curiously at Bobby. "What you mean you ain't afraid," he said. "What kind of nigga are you?"

"You guys mind your own business," Bobby said.

"Yes, sir," Darnell said.

"You are one dead nigger," Tyrone said. "They gonna fry yo black ass up at Raiford."

Bobby didn't reply.

"You think you a bad nigger?" Tyrone asked.

Again, Bobby didn't reply.

Ten minutes later, Bobby could hear the motor of the jail elevator. Moments later, a trusty, a young white man, entered the cell corridor, pushing a cart of food. He served Darnell and Tyrone, then turned to Bobby.

"You the one that killed the judge?" he asked.

Bobby ignored the question.

"You got some food for me?" Bobby asked.

"Yeah," he replied, shoving a tray through the food slot. "I hope you choke to death on it."

Breakfast was macaroni and cheese with fried bologna sandwiches and water. Bobby hadn't eaten since the day before, so he quickly wolfed down the food. Once finished, he turned and peered through the wire mesh over the window. Outside, he could see scrub jays skittering among the branches of the melaleuca trees. To the south, he could see part of downtown Wakoola Springs, the City Hall, the Piggly Wiggly supermarket, and the Woolworth five and dime. In the distance, he could see the Indian River, the ocean, and the sugar mill. He wondered what was happening at the sugar mill.

Around 9:30, he heard footsteps in the stairwell.

The door to the cellblock opened. A deputy appeared.

"Lincoln," he said. "Bobby Lincoln."

"That's me!"

"You going to see your lawyer."

Arraignment

Bobby's public defender was a man named Bill Hollis. In his late fifties, he was medium height, maybe five eight, with sad eyes and a gaunt, frail appearance. The lines in his face and the brown stains on his fingers testified to many nights of smoking and drinking. He had been on probation with the Florida Bar Association three years earlier after he was convicted of a driving and drinking charge. Despite this, he had a sincere smile and an understanding twinkle in his eye. His thinning, black hair was combed straight back, but some strands always seemed to fall over his eyes. When Bobby entered the detention room on the jail's second floor, Bill was waiting.

"I'm here to help you," he began. "You know this is going to be an uphill battle. Here you are, a black man that killed two white people."

Bobby nodded.

"I wouldn't get my hopes up too much if I was you."

"You make it sound like I'm already convicted," Bobby said.

"Well, I don't mean to," he said, brushing back his hair. "We can still put together a case. Tell me what happened."

Over the next thirty minutes, Bobby narrated the murders and surrounding circumstances. All the while, Bill was taking notes.

"Don't mention anything about the bootleg boat during the interview," he said. "That's a new charge. You don't want to incriminate yourself any more than you have already."

Bobby nodded.

"When they ask questions, stick with information about the murders. Don't volunteer anything!"

Bobby nodded.

"You understand the interview makes your confession official," he said. "Are you ready?"

Bobby nodded.

Moments later, four new people came into the detention room. There were two county detectives, an assistant district attorney, and a court stenographer with a reel-to-reel recording device. Over the next hour, as the plastic spools whirled on the upright reel-to-reel recorder, Bobby related the story of the murders again. All the while, the others took notes. Once Bobby was finished, the others asked questions. The detectives asked about the description of the boat, what color clothes they were wearing, whether the moon was out, where there would be fingerprints, what Lucky's demeanor was during the murders, as well as questions about Bobby's background with Lucky. Several times, the public defender instructed Bobby to not answer questions about his association with Carmelo's or his knowledge of what they called "the moonshine operation." Finally, after two hours, the interview was finished and Bobby was asked to sign papers stating that his testimony during the proceeding was true and correct. Once that was finished, Bobby and the PD were left alone in the detention room.

"How'd I do?" Bobby asked.

"You did fine," the PD said. "How do you want to plead?"

"I confessed," Bobby said.

"I know that," Bill said, "but you can still enter a not guilty plea."

"I don't know much about law," Bobby said.

For a long moment, the PD didn't answer.

"How old is this Floyd Holzafel?"

"Somewhere around fifty," Bobby replied.

"And you're twenty-four?"

Bobby nodded.

"We may be able to build a case claiming that you were led into the murders by an older white man you owed money to. We will argue that he influenced you to do things you would not normally have done."

"That's what happened," Bobby said.

Bill peered at his client.

"Even then, you could still get the death penalty."

Bobby didn't reply

"Of course, once you're convicted," the public defender continued, "it takes some time before the event actually occurs. Sometimes even years."

"So what should I do?" Bobby said.

"You should plead not guilty by reason of insanity," Bill said. "That's probably going to be the best case we can put together."

"If you say so," Bobby said.

"That's what we'll go with at the arraignment."

Bobby nodded.

"Arraignment is Tuesday," Bill said.

***

That night, back in his cell, Bobby lay awake, wondering what it would be like to die. He remembered watching Calvin die in Korea. The memory of the incident was always present in the back of his mind. Three separate times, Bobby, Calvin, and the other members of the all-Negro 24th Infantry Regiment had successfully defended the valley North of Pusan against

Chinese human wave attacks. During the fourth attack, Bobby and Calvin's machine gun position was overrun, and for more than twenty minutes, Bobby and the other members of the 24th were fighting enemy troops hand-to-hand. Finally, the Chinese retreated and a celebratory yell went up. The battle was over. Bobby looked down and saw that the outside of his left leg had been sliced open with a bayonet, but he was alive. Then he saw Calvin lying on the ground, slumped over an ammunition box.

"Cal! Cal!" Bobby said.

He rushed to his old friend.

Calvin's helmet was off, blood was streaming out of his nose, and his entire chest was a ragged mess. Bobby could see one of Calvin's lungs inflating and deflating like a toy balloon. It crossed his mind to call a medic, but he knew a medic could do nothing. Quickly, Bobby seated himself on the ground beside his old friend, then took his head under his arm and looked into his eyes.

Calvin slowly strained to raise his face to Bobby.

"I'm checking out," he said.

Bobby nodded. He knew there was nothing to say.

"Take care of yourself," Calvin said.

"I will," Bobby replied.

"Thanks for being my friend all these days."

"Thank you too, Cal."

Bobby offered his hand. Slowly, Calvin raised his hand, took Bobby's hand in his, and squeezed it for a brief second. Then Calvin's hand went limp. Just like that, his old friend was gone. Death was just a sudden, sure motion, Bobby reasoned, like changing lanes in traffic. Like you flip off a switch. Sort of like jerking a handkerchief out of your pocket.

***

The following morning, Bobby was awakened by the sound of scrub jays in the melaleuca trees. After he had eaten and washed, he waited for the deputies. This was the day of his arraignment. Shortly after ten a.m., he heard the deputies coming up the stairs.

Moments later, Bobby was shackled, then led out of the cellblock and down the stairwell. Even before he exited the side door to the courthouse walkway, he could hear loud voices. Once the door was opened, a chorus of shouting voices filled the air. Outside, some thirty or forty angry white men had gathered along the walkway.

"There he is!" one man said. "Hang him."

"Kill that nigger."

"You as good as dead!" another man shouted, waving his fist.

"They gonna fry you, nigger!"

The two deputies pushed aside the crowd to make way for themselves and Bobby. As the crowd parted, news photographers suddenly rushed in and the flashes of light momentarily caused Bobby to lose his vision. Moments later, Bobby and the deputies were inside the courthouse hallway. As they passed, there were more angry shouts, then they entered the courtroom.

Inside the courtroom, a hubbub of voices filled the air as Bobby was led down the center aisle to a counsel table. In the jammed wooden pews, spectators strained to get a glimpse of the man who had killed their judge. Ahead, Bobby could see his public defender waiting. Moments later, as Bobby was unchained and seated, the hubbub of voices grew louder.

"Order!" the judge barked, rapping his gavel.

The crowd grew quiet and the judge turned to some papers before him. Bobby peered across the courtroom. Never in his life had he had so many people staring at him. He glanced up to the balcony. He saw his mother and Clifford seated among the spectators. He was ashamed for his mother to see him.

"William Robert Lincoln," the judge said, his voice booming across the courtroom. "You have been charged with two counts of capital murder in the deaths of Judge Harold Chillingsworth and his wife Margaret. How do you plead?"

"Not guilty by reason of insanity," Bobby said.

A ripple of oohs and ahhs waved across the crowd.

"Order!" the judge said.

"Let the defendant's plea be noted in the record," the judge said. "Bond has been set at $250,000 and trial will be held April 3, 1956. Anything further?"

"No, your honor," Bill said.

"Court dismissed," the judge said.

The entire affair had lasted five minutes.

Back in the detention room, the public defender had some parting words for Bobby.

"Well, it's going to be six months before the trial," he said. "I would try to get used to jail life. Maybe by then, we can get some idea of how the prosecutors are going to proceed. I'd just try to make the best I could of the jail time until the trial. You'll be all right in jail. The food is not worth a damn, but you got a warm, dry place to sleep every night. It would be best if you didn't fraternize with any of the other prisoners."

"Why do you say that?"

"Because right now, you're the most famous Negro in Wakoola County," Bill said. "I'm sure there's more than a few young ones in that jail that would love to take you down a notch or two."

"So I'll have my own cell?"

"Looks that way," Bill said. "Sheriff wanted it that way."

Bags Calhoun

The following morning, Bobby had eaten, done his daily business, and was trying to decide how to occupy himself. He had been behind bars four days and already he could see the biggest problem he was going to have was the boredom. He needed something to occupy his mind. Across the way, Darnell and Tyrone were playing spades. Suddenly, Bobby heard the whirring sound of the motor on the elevator. The elevator, built adjacent to the stairs, was used to move prisoners who were in a wheelchair. When the elevator door opened, the sound of squeaking wheels filled the corridor and Bobby saw an old Negro man pushing a cart. Once the cart was off the elevator, the old man pushed a button and, seconds later, the cart and the old man were inside the cellblock.

"Morning, Bags," said Darnell.

The old man smiled.

"Morning, Darnell," he replied.

"Bags" Calhoun was a slow-moving Negro man in his late sixties, slightly hunched over and wearing wire-rimmed glasses and a cap. Around the edges of the cap were tufts of snow-white hair. The bags under his eyes testified to too many years of late night reading and had won him his nickname. The cart he was pushing was stacked high with books. He glanced over and saw Bobby.

"I see we got a new member in the club," he said with a big smile.

Bobby smiled.

"Name's Bobby," he said.

"How you doing?" the old man replied. "The boys downstairs told me you were up here. You confessed to the Chillingsworth murders?"

Bobby nodded.

"You may be behind bars for a long time," Bags said.

"That's what they tell me," Bobby replied. "What you got there?"

"Books. All kind of books," the old man said. "You like to read?"

"I liked to read when I was younger," he said. "I just never seem to be able to find the time."

"You got time now," Bags said. "What you interested in?"

Bobby peered at the cart. He saw a copy of *Ferdinand the Bull* and *Bambi*.

"You got books on there for little kids."

"Some people behind these bars can barely read," Bags said.

"Got anything about good and evil?" Bobby asked.

Bags laughed, turned to the cart, and picked up a copy of the Bible.

"I got this," he said. "It's the most famous book on that subject I know of. But if this one don't move you, there are other avenues."

"What would you recommend other than that one?" Bobby asked.

"Well, you could start with Aristotle and Plato. Lots has been written about morals. Usually morals are an outgrowth of religion. One religion will have one set of morals and another religion will have another."

Bobby remembered his master sergeant in Korea.

"What about General Patton?" Bobby said. "Got anything on General Patton?"

"You want something about his life or his exploits?"

"His what?"

"His exploits," Bags said. You want to know about his personal life or his accomplishments?"

"Both," Bobby said.

Bags turned and dug through the books. Moments later, he pulled out a dusty tome with a ragged cover.

"Patton's battle strategies," he said, handing it to Bobby.

Bobby examined the book.

"Yeah," he said. "That will get me started. What else you got?"

"Lots of law books," Bags said. "Plenty of jailhouse lawyers pass through these bars. Court procedures, rules of evidence, discovery, motions... I've read lots of these myself."

Bobby shook his head.

"Maybe later," he said. "Let me see how I do with this one."

"I can get you most anything you want," he said. "If I ain't got it on the cart, I can usually get it from the county bookmobile. It comes every Thursday."

"What about the history of God?"

"You're going for some heavy duty material," Bags said. "I do have a book in my cell about the origins of God."

"Can you bring it?"

"I can do that," he said.

Bags looked across the way to the other two inmates playing cards.

"What about you, Darnell?" Bags said. "Anything you want?"

"Got any pictures of naked women?" Darnell said.

"Not today," Bags said. "They won't let me have something like that. Tyrone?" Bags asked. "Anything you want?"

Tyrone looked up from his spades hand.

"I want you to get some oil for the wheels on that damn thing."

Bags didn't reply.

"See y'all later," he said, then he started pushing the cart of books across the concrete floor to the next cellblock.

Bobby sat down on his bunk and opened the book. Outside the window, he could hear two Florida woodpeckers tapping away in one of the melaleuca trees. Bobby glanced through the chapter headings. There were chapters on Patton's campaign in Italy, others on the retaking of France, especially the Battle of the Bulge, and still others on the D-Day invasion. Each chapter contained detailed explanations and drawings of Patton's tank battle strategies. Finally, he settled down to the chapters on the Battle of the Bulge. The narrative listed in great detail how Patton believed that the key to winning battles was to know everything you could about your enemy. His personal likes, dislikes, education, artistic influences, family, even his favorite foods. Patton believed any of these details could provide clues to help predict what his enemy would do in battle.

Over the next three days, Bobby pored over the book. As he read, he came across numerous words he didn't understand. Using the paper and pencil he received in his personal jail packet, he made a list. He would ask Bags about the words.

***

The following Tuesday, Bags was back. Over the past four days, Bobby had read the Patton book three times and he was anxious to get the book on God.

"How'd you like the Patton book?"

"I liked it," Bobby said. "I just didn't understand all of the words."

"Here you go," Bags said, handing him the new book.

Bobby looked at it. The title read *What is God?*

"Bags, I guess you've done lots of reading and know the meaning of lots of words."

"Yeah," Bags said "Why do you ask?"

"I got a bunch of words here I don't know what they mean."

He showed the list to Bags. Bags took it.

The words animosity, circumlocution, intrigue, conundrum, and waif had been scribbled on the paper.

"What is that first word?" Bobby asked. "What is animosity?"

"Animosity is when somebody don't like somebody else," Bags said. "If you have animosity for somebody, it means you don't like them; you hate them."

"Okay," Bobby said. "What about that next word.... circumlocution?"

"Circumlocution is when someone talks around a subject," Bags said. "They don't address the subject directly…"

The old man stopped and turned back to the cart.

"Here!" he said, taking a book from the cart. "Here's what you need."

Bobby took the book and examined it.

"It's called a dictionary," Bags said. "If you don't understand a word, you look it up. If you make a note of what it means, you'll know what it is next time."

Bobby thumbed through the pages.

"If you learn ten words a day," Bags continued, "you'll know lots of words before you know it. The more words you know, the better reader you become."

Bobby was impressed.

"You got any books about the way the world was created? Not what the Bible says. A scientific explanation."

"There are lots of books on the bookmobile about evolution and geology and biology," Bags said. "I do have a book on high school biology."

Bags took a book from the cart and handed it to Bobby.

Bobby thumbed through the pages.

"Yeah," Bobby said. "This will get me started. Next time, bring me a book about geology. Geology is about rocks and stuff? Right?"

"That's right," Bags said. "But there are lots of ologies. Each of them is a specific field of study. There is biology, the study of living things, geology, the study of the earth, psychology, the study of the human mind, anthropology, the study of man, physiology, the human body, immunology…"

"Whoa! Whoa!!" Bobby interrupted.

Bags stopped.

"You know," Bobby said. "You are one smart man."

"I've read lots of books," Bags replied.

"Do you know who Carl Jung was?"

"He was a psychologist," Bags said with a professorial air. "He believed that the driving force in human beings was the herding instinct… the need to socialize."

When Bags spoke, he had the bearing of a professor. There was authority in his voice and a certainty to his tone.

"The big three in psychology," Bags continued, "was Freud, Adler, and Jung. Freud believed the basis of all human action was sexual in nature. Adler believed human's basic motive was feelings of inferiority. Jung believed it was the need to belong to a group."

He paused.

Bobby considered his words.

"You know, all of life is in the human mind," Bobby said. "If you understood the workings of the human mind, you should be able to understand why everything on this earth was ever done."

"It's not quite that simple," Bags said. "The human mind is a dark forest. From a distance, it all looks cut and dried, but when you examine it closely, the human mind is a battlefield. There is no single dimension of the human mind which doesn't have an opposite. Good and evil, love and hate, black and white, greed and charity... All of them are in there together."

He paused.

"You looking for a book on psychology?"

"Yeah," Bobby said. "Bring me what you got."

"Hey!" Tyrone interrupted from across the cell corridor. "Y'all shut up all that stupid jabbering. I'm trying to play cards over here."

Bags winked at Bobby.

"See you next time," Bags said.

Then he started pushing the cart across the concrete floor, its wheels making an agonizing, screeching sound.

"Do something about them God-damned wheels," Tyrone shouted as Bags moved to the next cellblock.

Answers

All that day and into the night, Bobby spent reading the book on the nature of God. It explained the origins of a supreme being in human history, early concepts of God, and the major religions of the world, including Christianity, Catholicism, Islam, and the various Asiatic religions. Again, there were words Bobby didn't understand. Monotheistic, covenants, epistemology, and others. As Bobby came across each word that he didn't understand, he made a note of it. At the end of every day, he would go through the dictionary, find the meaning, make a note, and memorize the meaning of the word. Bobby's mind was expanding and the concept of God was becoming clearer to him.

***

The following Sunday, Bobby had a visitor. It was Clifford. The visiting room was like a teller's windows in a bank. The inmate and the visitor sat across from one another, a thick glass divider between them.

There was a small, filtered opening in the glass divider through which voices could pass. Bobby was glad to see his old friend.

"Look at this!" Clifford said, holding a copy of the *County Clarion*. The banner headline read: "Negro Confesses to

Chillingsworth Murders" Directly underneath was a photo of Bobby in jail stripes being led into court.

"You're famous," Clifford said. "Everybody in Wakoola County knows who Bobby Lincoln is now."

"I'm not sure that's something to be proud of," Bobby said. "How's Mama doing?"

"She's fine," Clifford said. "She just worries about you all the time. She sent some apple pie, but they wouldn't let me bring it in."

"And you," Bobby asked. "You doing okay?"

"I'm okay," Clifford said. "I have to tell you jail has been good for you. You look a lot better than you did a couple weeks ago."

"I feel a lot better too," Bobby said.

Clifford studied his old friend.

"What do you think is going to happen to you?" he asked finally.

"I don't know," Bobby said. "Everybody is telling me I'm going to be behind bars for a long time."

Long pause.

"The boys down at the sugar mill was talking about you," Clifford said. "They hired a new man to run the rollers."

"How's Train doing?"

"I don't know," Clifford said. "I haven't seen him. He didn't show up for work one day last week and nobody has seen him since."

"He might be in jail," Bobby said.

"Lazarus wants to come see you."

"No," Bobby said. "I don't want him to see me in here. He looks up to me and I don't want to disappoint him."

"He knows what's happening," Clifford said. "When he first heard the news, he didn't believe it. 'No way Bobby Lincoln would kill somebody,' he said. 'Bobby is too good a person...'"

"Yeah," Bobby said. "I know he believes in me."

"He really wants to see you."

"No," Bobby said.

Another long pause.

"It don't look good for you, Bobby," Clifford said.

Bobby inhaled.

"I know," Bobby replied. "I'm going to take it one day at a time. That's all I can do."

"They got Lucky downstairs with the white folks," Clifford said. "They say he is not a happy camper."

Bobby laughed.

"Wait until this is over," Bobby said. "He's going to be unhappier than ever."

"You better watch yo'self," Clifford said. "You don't want to piss off nobody in here. They'll put a shiv in yo gut."

"I know how to take care of myself," Bobby said.

"Lucky's people, Carmelo and that bunch," Clifford said. "They know that if you confessed, you're probably going to testify for the state and send Lucky to the electric chair. No two ways about it. They don't want you testifying against Lucky."

"We'll see what happens," Bobby replied.

A deputy stepped forward.

"Time's up!" he said.

Clifford got up to go.

"Your mama sent some money for your commissary account," Clifford said. "I left it with one of the deputies."

"Thanks," Bobby said.

Then he watched as Clifford strolled back across the concrete floor and exited the door of the visitors' room.

***

When Bags arrived the following Tuesday morning, he had five new books for Bobby. There was a primer on Freudian psychology, a thick book on geology titled *Origins of the Earth*, a book on evolution titled *Evolution in Action*, and two books by anthropologist Margaret Mead.

All that day, Bobby pored over the biology book. He was mesmerized. As he read, he knew this was the information he had been seeking all of his life. All that night, he studied its pages, reading the concepts and studying the drawings that depicted the anatomy and classifications of plants, animals, birds, fishes, and insects. As he read, he surmised that all living creatures needed oxygen, food, an elimination system, and some method of procreation. He compared the skeletal structures of mammals, birds, and fish to that of humans. He concluded there was a general pattern – a template, so to speak – to the construction of all living things. As he studied the anatomy of humans, he realized that most creatures had the same basic components: a torso, a head, and arms and legs. Fins and wings served fish and birds in the same way arms and legs served human beings. The world was starting to make sense to Bobby.

***

Over the month of October, Bags visited Bobby's cellblock five separate times. Each time, Bobby would return several books and get a stack of new ones. During that month, he read a total of eight books. Books on psychology, geology, and anthropology. He especially enjoyed the works of Margaret Mead and Ruth Benedict.

During Bags' first visit in early November, he offered some advice.

158

"Now you know you haven't touched literature, history, and philosophy," Bags said. "If you want to be really well rounded, you're going to need those."

"History?" Bobby asked. "You got anything on Hannibal of Carthage?"

"Yep! Got two of them," Bags said. "I'll bring 'em next time."

The month of November and Thanksgiving came and went. During the month, Bobby read thirteen books, mostly literature, history, and philosophy. One book, the complete works of Shakespeare, he pored over for more than a week. At first, he stumbled over the old English words, trying to make sense of their meanings. Many times, he couldn't put an exact meaning to a word, but, after some analysis, he could usually understand the context of the sentence the word was being used in. After struggling through *Macbeth* and *Othello*, he had a fairly good understanding of the verbiage by the time he was ready to read *Hamlet*. Over the course of two days, he read *Hamlet* four times and memorized Hamlet's speech at Yorick's grave.

The following Tuesday when Bags arrived into the cellblock, Bobby wanted to demonstrate what he had learned. Once they had greeted one another, Bobby told Bags, "Check this out!"

Then, using a shaving mug as the skull of Yorick, he recited Hamlet's famous speech.

"Alas poor Yorick," Bobby said, peering intently at the shaving mug. "I knew him, Horatio, a fellow of infinite jest, of most excellent fancy. He hath borne me on his back a thousand times, and now, how abhorred in my imagination it is! My gorge rises at it."

Across the cell corridor, when Darnell heard Bobby speaking, he went to the bars and listened as Bobby addressed the shaving mug.

"Here hung those lips that I have kissed I know not how oft. —Where be your gibes now? Your gambols? Your songs? Your flashes of merriment that were wont to set the table on a roar? Not one now to mock your own grinning? Quite chapfallen? Now get you to my lady's chamber and tell her, let her paint an inch thick, to this favor she must come...."

"Bravo!! Bravo!!" Bags said, clapping his hands in pure delight.

Across the way, Darnell peered at Bobby in sheer disbelief. "You are one crazy nigga," he said.

***

During the month of December, Bobby read nineteen books. Now he was venturing into literature and poetry and philosophy. Each and every time he finished a book, he would make a note of questions he had for Bags. They were mostly philosophical questions about the nature of God, the origins of the universe, and the concept of time. Bobby knew if anyone was going to have honest, forthright answers to these questions, it would be Bags.

Three days before Christmas, Bobby had a new visitor. It was Idella. He was happy to see her, but, from the first, she seemed cold and distant.

"Why did you come here?" he asked.

"I asked myself the same question," she said. "I guess it's because I love you. You own a part of my heart and it is killing me to see you like this. Is there anything I can do?"

"Not really," he said. "You know all the details of my situation?"

"I know," she said. "I don't see how in the world you're going to get out of this."

Bobby studied her for a moment.

"I haven't forgotten you," he said. "When this is over, I'll contact you. Until then, there is no need for you to come here."

She didn't answer at first.

"From what I hear, you may never get out of jail," Idella said finally. "Some say you might even go to the electric chair."

Bobby didn't reply.

Suddenly, Idella burst into tears.

"There's no need for that," Bobby said. "I made this bed. Now I have to lie in it."

She looked away, then wiped her eyes with a handkerchief.

"I understand, Bobby," she said. "I understand your feelings. If you do want to contact me, I'll be at my mother's in Manatee."

"Thanks," Bobby replied.

"Bye," she said, standing up to leave.

"Bye," Bobby replied, then watched as Idella turned and started across the concrete floor to the visiting room door. As the door closed behind her, Bobby wanted to cry.

Christmas Conversation

On Christmas day, Bobby had the entire cellblock to himself. Two days earlier, Darnell had been transferred to Tallahassee to start his sentence and the irritable Tyrone had been gone for over two weeks. Bobby loved the peace and quiet, especially now that he spent all of his time reading. Through the wire mesh, he could see the deserted streets of Wakoola Springs below him. Now that Christmas day had arrived, all the stores were closed and the streets were deserted. Christmas decorations on streetlights, trees, and the business fronts remained in place. Somewhere in the distance, Bobby could hear the tinkle of a Salvation Army bell and a chorus singing "Silent Night." He was waiting on Bags. The old man said he would visit Bobby on Christmas day and they could talk as long as they liked.

When Bags arrived that afternoon, Bobby was waiting. He had several questions he wanted to ask, but he wanted to get his new books first.

"What you got?" Bobby asked when Bags stopped the cart in front of his cell.

"Two more books on philosophy, Shelley's poems, and Plato's *Republic,*" Bags said, passing the books through the bars.

"Read this one very closely," Bags said, indicating Plato's *Republic*. "Some of the most important knowledge in the world is in here."

"Why do you say that?"

"Times change, but people don't," Bags said. "All the knowledge in that book is just as relevant today as it was 2000 years ago."

"Like what?"

"Read it. Read it for yourself and understand it," Bags said. "Then we'll talk about it."

Bobby put the books on his bunk.

"Now let's talk about you," Bobby said.

"What you want to know?"

"First of all, what you in for?"

Bags smiled and peered for a long moment at Bobby. Then he spoke.

"I killed my wife and my best friend."

"Why?"

"I caught 'em in flagrant delecti."

"That sounds serious," Bobby said.

"It was dead serious for me," Bags said. "One afternoon, I come home from work early. When I went in the house, I thought I heard something in the bedroom, then I hear the bed springs going. I knew what was going on, so I slipped into the other bedroom and got my .38. He was on top of her when I blowed his brains out all over the picture of Christ hanging over the bed. After I killed him, I told her to pray, but she jumped up and started running. I shot her once in the back and followed her to the porch. She died crawling down the steps…"

Bobby looked at him and shook his head in amazement.

"That's quite a story, Bags," Bobby said.

"And do you know what's funny?"

"What's that?"

"If I had it to do all over again, I would do the same thing."

The old man slapped his thigh with joyous laughter.

"They gave me two life sentences," he continued, "but that was commuted to seventy-five years when Truman came in. In 1951, after thirty-eight years at Raiford, the parole board said I was no longer a threat to society, so they transferred me to Wakoola County."

"Why here?"

"I asked for Wakoola," he said. "I know this woman out at Blue Springs they let come visit me once a week. At seventy-one, I don't need a woman like I did when I was younger."

Bags took off his cap and scratched his head. His hair was snowy white.

"You know, Bobby," he said. "After you spend thirty-eight years behind bars, you learn to handle just about anything life throws at you. There ain't nothing that can hurt you anymore."

Bags paused.

"Let me ask you something else," Bobby said. "What do you think happens to you when you die?"

"You want the official version or the personal version?"

"Personal version," Bobby said.

He looked at Bobby for a long moment before speaking.

"Science teaches that energy is neither created nor destroyed," he said with a certain professorial air. "It just changes form. If you freeze water, you got ice. If you boil it, it disappears into the air. The substance remains the same; only the form changes."

He stopped. His eyes started to fill with tears.

"When my younger brother died…"

"You lost a brother, Bags?" Bobby asked.

"Yes, I did!" the old man replied, wiping his tears on his shirtsleeve. "Me and Larry were working together on a construction project in Miami. We had poured two concrete floors – probably two tons of wet concrete – to build the second floor. Moments after the truck left, the forms started to give out under the weight of all that concrete. When I heard

164

the forms start to crack, I yelled to my brother, who was pulling wire on the first floor. 'Go on, Larry! Get out!' He looked up and saw the floor above him was falling down, but it was too late. The entire concrete floor crashed down on top of him. I knew he was dead before I went to him. As I watched, a green smoke arose atop the pile of wet concrete and broken forms. That green smoke, it was like a mist in a valley in the afternoon, was my brother's spirit passing to the great beyond."

Bags stopped, then he put his elbows on his knees, buried his face in his hands, and started to sob. Bobby's eyes filled with tears as he watched his good friend in his grief. Finally, Bags stopped weeping and wiped his eyes.

"I guess one of the reasons why I enjoyed talking to you so much is because my brother was about your age when he died."

"I'm sorry, Bags," Bobby said.

"That's okay," Bags replied. "It always hurts me when I think about him. At first, I didn't think I was going to get over it. But I did. I've made it this far."

Bobby took a deep breath.

"You know, Bags, you're the smartest man I have ever known."

"I've spent lots of time reading books," Bags replied.

"I've got a friend that says you don't know how smart you are until you start to read."

"That pretty well sums it up," he said. "Nothing grows you as a person like reading."

"Don't you ever want to get out of here?"

The old man pursed his lips and shook his head.

"Not really," he said. "If I was outside, I couldn't get a job reading and talking to people all day about books. Way it is now, I get to explore 'the realms of gold' and have a nice, quiet place to lay my head every night."

"Realms of gold?" Bobby asked.

"You know, intellectual stuff."

Bags and Bobby talked for almost three hours that Christmas Day. When Bags left, he offered his hand. Bobby shook it. He loved his conversations with Bags. The old man was a treasure trove of information on every subject under the sun. For any question Bobby had, Bags always had a ready and clear answer. Every time he talked to Bags, he always felt larger inside himself and found something new and different to add to the welter of his growing mind. When Bags left that afternoon, Bobby watched as the old man shuffled back across the jail corridor, pushing the cart. As he watched, he thought to himself how fortunate he had been to have met him. Bags was making a totally new person out of him. It had been a wonderful afternoon.

District Attorney

Glenn O'Donnell, the District Attorney in Wakoola County, was a medium height, stocky man in his late forties who had the constant scowl of an angry bulldog. An attorney in Wakoola Springs for eighteen years, he had been elected to the prosecutor's post four years earlier, promising to clean up corruption. A Catholic layman, he had been a professional welterweight prizefighter at one time and the misalignment of his nose bridge was testimony to that fact. Married with two teenage children, he was known as a tough, all-business prosecutor who always went by the book. When he called Sheriff Cunningham into his office that afternoon, he came straight to the point.

"Sam," the DA said, "I want to win this Chillingsworth case more than any case I've ever had in my life. This is not only the biggest murder case to ever hit Wakoola County, but my entire legacy hinges on the outcome. Whatever it takes to win this case and get the responsible parties convicted, I'm going to do it."

"I know how important it is," the sheriff said.

"Only problem is I don't have a starting point to build a case," the DA said. "I don't have a body, no witnesses, no leads, no evidence... not diddly squat to build a case on."

"How can I help?"

"This Negro you have in jail," the prosecutor began, "this William Robert Lincoln that made the confession... What do you know about him?"

The sheriff explained he had known Bobby since he was a young boy. He explained that his father worked for his demolition company before he got into politics and had once saved his life. The DA listened silently as the sheriff recited the history of his relationship with Bobby. Finally, when he had finished, the DA studied him for a long moment.

"What are you driving at, Glenn?" the sheriff said finally.

"If this Negro wanted to become a state witness," he said, "I would have a starting point for a case. I would have information to investigate and leads to follow. Basically, I think I could probably get to the bottom of what happened to Judge Chillingsworth and his wife."

The sheriff inhaled.

"What would be in it for Bobby?"

"If he has a clear record and is a credible witness, I could negotiate a plea deal and probably get him off with a light sentence. On the other hand, if he is a career criminal who has been in and out of jail all of his life and is not credible, then that's another story."

"Oh, Bobby has a good record," the sheriff said. "I know that. You want to talk to him?"

"Yeah," the DA said with a nod. "Bring him in."

***

The following morning, Bobby woke up to the sound of lawn mowers. Maintenance workers were mowing the grass on the south side of the jail. As they mowed, a flock of white spoonbills—some twenty or thirty strong—were cautiously following the mowers, intermittently plucking insects out of the newly mown grass. To the south, along Dixie Highway,

Bobby could see big trucks going north, hauling loads of oranges and grapefruits. Tourists in sedans and convertibles headed south to Miami to spend their vacation money. Today, he would read *The Age of Reason*, the works of Kant and Descartes. It was slow going and there were long words he didn't understand. Every few minutes, he would have to stop and check the dictionary.

Once he had eaten and washed, he settled into the book, then he heard footsteps and voices in the stairwell. Moments later, two deputies appeared.

"Lincoln!" one called as they entered the cell block.

Bobby turned.

"Sheriff wants to see you," one deputy said.

Moments later, Bobby was shackled, then led down the stairs to the second-floor detention room. As he walked, he wondered why the sheriff would want to see him. His trial was still three months away.

The sheriff was waiting.

"Sit down, Bobby," the sheriff said.

Bobby took a seat.

"There may be a chance for you to get out of this," he said.

Bobby peered curiously at him.

"What you talking about, sheriff?"

"You need to talk to the DA," the sheriff said. "You might have a miracle waiting on your doorstep."

"What's going on?" Bobby asked again.

"I'm afraid I might say the wrong thing," the sheriff said. "Just go and talk to the DA. He wants to talk to you."

"When?" Bobby asked.

"This afternoon."

"Don't I need to talk to the public defender first?"

"No," the sheriff said. "I already talked to him."

***

169

That afternoon, a deputy escorted Bobby from the jail to the DA's office in the courthouse. When the deputy opened the door to the office, the DA looked up, saw Bobby and the deputy, and motioned them in.

"Take off the shackles and wait outside," he said.

Moments later, Bobby was seated. He rubbed his wrists to relieve the soreness of the metal handcuffs. He waited for the DA to speak first.

"Go on; sit down, boy," the DA said.

Bobby took a seat in front of the desk.

"Bobby?" the DA began. "Can I call you Bobby?"

"That's fine," Bobby said. "I like that better than 'boy.'"

The DA scowled at Bobby's comment, then started again.

"You know," the DA said. "You're in lots of trouble here. You are a Negro that has confessed to the killing of two white people. Not just two ordinary white people, but a County Circuit Judge and his wife."

Bobby nodded.

"I guess you know," the DA continued, "you might very well end up in the electric chair."

Bobby nodded.

The DA studied him.

"Didn't yo mama never taught you that it was wrong to go out and kill another person?"

"Why you ask me that?"

"Because I want to know," the DA said.

Bobby didn't answer at first.

"I had a good mama," he said finally. "She tried to teach me the difference between right and wrong."

"You ever been arrested before?"

Bobby shook his head.

"How much education you had, boy?" the DA asked.

"I finished high school in the army," Bobby replied.

The DA peered at him. A long, silent pause.

"I've listened to your confession," the DA said. "Three different times. I have every reason to believe you are telling the truth..."

Bobby interrupted.

"What do you want from me?" he asked. "Why did you call me in here?"

"I wanted to make you an offer," the DA said. "An offer that might save you from the electric chair."

Bobby perked up.

"Are you playing with me?"

"No, I'm very serious."

"Then what's your offer?" Bobby said.

The DA inhaled.

"I got a problem prosecuting this case," he said. "I can't go to trial until I have direct evidence to present to a jury. I don't have a corpus delecti."

"A what?"

"A corpus delecti," the DA said. "A body. I can't prove a murder without a body. So I've got to have a witness to the murder before I got a case. I want to know if you would be interested in becoming a state's witness and work with me in getting a conviction."

"A conviction against who?"

"Floyd George Holzafel," the DA replied. "The man you claim led you into the murders."

"I believe that's called 'copping a plea,'" Bobby said.

"That's right," the DA said. "If you want to work with me and tell me everything you know about the case – the people involved, their motives and circumstances – I could probably get you off with a light sentence."

"How light?"

"Five years," the DA replied.

Bobby didn't answer.

"It's a matter of you help me and I help you," the DA said. "You scratch my back and I'll scratch yours. I want to help you, boy."

Bobby laughed out loud.

"No," he said. "You want to help yourself."

The DA stopped. His face took on another angry scowl. "What you laughing at, boy?" the DA asked. "This is not some game we're playing here. Your life is at stake. Don't you understand the seriousness of all this?"

Bobby studied the DA without speaking.

"So what do you say?" the DA said finally.

"You're not helping your cause by the way you're treating me."

"What?" the DA replied. "What you talking about?"

"Calling me boy and looking down on me."

"Who the hell you think you talking to?" he asked. "Do you know who I am? I'm the number one law enforcer in this county. Why, I could send you to the electric chair by just signing my name."

"Not without a trial first," Bobby replied.

The DA was now livid.

"Now listen to me, boy," the DA added.

"Are we finished?"

The white man peered disbelievingly at the Negro.

"What kind of Negro are you?"

"I've got nothing else to say," Bobby said.

The DA peered at him.

"Now ain't that just like a Negro," he said. "Try to help them and they get uppity. Well, you ain't gonna treat me like that, boy."

He stood up behind the desk.

"Do you understand?" he said. "I'm a white man and you don't talk to me like that!"

Bobby didn't reply.

"Deputy!" the DA called.

The office door opened and the deputy peeked inside.

"Take the prisoner back to jail."

***

The following Tuesday morning, Bags made his regular visit. Once Bobby had received his new books, one on physics and another on astronomy, he mentioned the DA's offer. After hearing the offer, Bags pondered for a moment.

"I can see the DA's position," he said. "He's got nothing. There was a murder case in Tampa eight or nine years ago... I believe it was *State of Florida vs. Foster*. The prosecutor didn't have a body or evidence, but there was a witness, one of the accomplices to the murder. As I recall, the accomplice turned state's evidence and got off scot-free."

"What should I do?" Bobby asked.

Bags smiled.

"I certainly wouldn't give up a chance to escape the electric chair," Bags said. "We're talking about your life here. Or even a long prison term, but knowing Glenn O'Donnell, he's going to make you serve a little time if you agree to his offer. Even if it's a year. If you play your cards right, you can probably get off scot-free."

Bags stopped and absently peered at the concrete floor.

"You got him over a barrel," Bags said. "He wants this conviction and he wants it bad. Stick by your guns. Hold out for total freedom."

Bobby pursed his lips.

"Also, make sure he promises not to prosecute for your moonshining activities. If there is anything he can use to get you in prison for a while, he'll do it. Like I said, stick by your guns."

New Negotiations

On Monday of the following week, around midmorning, the prisoners heard footsteps coming up the stairwell. It was a deputy.

"Bobby Lincoln," he said. "The DA wants to talk to you again."

Fifteen minutes later, Bobby was back in the DA's office.

Once Bobby was unchained and the deputy disappeared, the district attorney peered at Bobby for a long moment as if he were trying to solve a puzzle. Finally, he spoke.

"How you doing today, Bobby?" he asked.

His tone was not as harsh as before.

"I'm doing okay," Bobby replied.

"From your record, I see you served in Korea."

Bobby nodded.

"Four years with the 24th Infantry Regiment," he said. "My best friend was killed in a human wave attack North of Pusan."

For a long moment, he peered studiously at Bobby, then abruptly stood up and started staring out the window behind him.

"That's highly commendable," he said thoughtfully. "I didn't serve myself. They turned me down because I had a heart murmur. Sometimes, I wish I had. Serving your country is something a man can be proud of."

Bobby nodded.

"I been thinking about what you said," the DA continued. "Maybe I was a little hasty, a little presumptuous last time. I want to try again to see if we can work together."

Bobby didn't reply.

"Can we be friends, Bobby?"

Bobby sat silently.

"What can I do to get your cooperation on this?"

Bobby inhaled.

"Go ahead," the DA said. "Tell me what's on your mind."

"Don't get me wrong," Bobby began. "I'd like to have my life and freedom as much as the next man and part of me would be happy to work with you. On the other hand, I don't want to deal with being called 'boy' every time I turn around. You look down on me like I was a dog. You're no better than I am. I'm a human being just like you. I want to be treated with respect."

"So what do you want me to do?"

"Tell you what," Bobby said. "You start treating me like I was a white man and I'll help you convict Lucky."

"What you talking about?"

"Stop looking down on me," Bobby said. "Yes, I'm a Negro, but I'm not necessarily lazy and ignorant and have no ambition. You don't know anything about who I really am. All you see is this black skin and everything you say to me is part of that."

A long silence. The district attorney turned from Bobby and peered out the window at the street below.

"Look down there at that brown dog doing his business on that fire hydrant," the DA said. "Come over here, Bobby, and look at this."

Bobby got up from the chair and walked behind the desk. Down below, Bobby could see a dog was finishing his business. Then he watched as it trotted off down the street.

"Every Thursday morning around 9:30, that dog does his business on that fire hydrant. It's just like he don't know nothing else."

"What's that got to do with our conversation?"

"In some ways, I'm like that dog," the DA said. "I don't really want to be mean or look down on anybody, but my attitude toward blacks has been inbred in me for so long, I'm not sure I can change."

"If I'm going to work with you, I want to be treated as your equal," Bobby said. "That's not too much to ask."

"Maybe you're right," the DA said. "So what can I do?"

"When I come into your office, say 'Good morning, Mr. Lincoln.'

"Step out from behind your desk and shake my hand. Then say to me, please be seated. Treat me like I'm intelligent and know what's going on in the world. And don't call me 'boy.' That's treating me like I was your dog. I'm not your dog."

The DA pursed his lips and considered Bobby's words.

"Okay," he said finally. "I get your point. If I change my attitude, will you work with me?"

"Not so fast," Bobby said. "What are you going to do for me?"

"Well, I can get you a light sentence for your testimony."

"What do you call light?"

"Five years."

Bobby shook his head.

"No," he said. "If you want my cooperation, I want total immunity."

"You've got to serve some time," the DA said. "You're a black man that helped kill two white people. I can't let you walk out of here scot-free."

"If you want me to work with you, you will."

The DA shook his head.

"You drive a hard bargain," he said. "Tell you what, you help me convict Holzafel and find out who wanted the judge and his wife killed, and I'll take your jail time down to a year."

"What else do you want?" Bobby said. "You got my confession."

"No, I've got to know who Lucky was working for. Somebody paid him to have the judge and his wife killed. Did he tell you who that was?"

"No," Bobby said. "I asked, but he wouldn't tell me."

"I've got to have that for the case," the DA said. "The case is basically not finished until I have a motive."

"I might be able to help you with that," Bobby said. "I know a man that knows a lot about the gambling and moonshine operations up and down this coast."

The DA didn't answer. He was weighing Bobby's offer.

"So what do you say?" Bobby said finally.

"Okay. God damn it," the DA said. "If you help me convict Lucky and find out who wanted the judge and his wife dead, I'll let you go scot-free."

"What about the moonshining?" Bobby said. "No prosecution on that too?"

"No prosecution."

"And you'll put it in writing?"

"I'll put it in writing," the DA said.

Bobby smiled.

"Then let's get down to business," the DA said.

"No," Bobby said, "not so fast. I want you to prove to me you can treat me like I'm a white man. Tomorrow, I'll come back to your office and I want to see you treat me as your equal."

"Okay," the DA said. "What time?"

"Ten a.m."

"I'll be waiting," the DA said.

Investigation

The following morning, promptly at 9:45, the deputy returned to Bobby's cellblock, then, ten minutes later, they were back in the DA's office.

Once Bobby appeared in the office, the shackles were removed and the deputy disappeared.

"Good morning, Mr. Lincoln," the DA said.

"Good morning, sir," Bobby replied.

Instantly, the DA arose, walked around his desk, and offered his hand. Bobby shook his hand.

"Please be seated," the DA said.

Bobby took a seat, then the DA walked back around the desk and seated himself again.

"How did I do?" he said.

"Pretty good!" Bobby said. "In fact, damn good... Thanks for treating me like the human being I am. Okay. Let's get started."

"Let me set up a tape recorder," the DA said. Moments later, the same reel-to-reel recorder that was used during the confession was in place. Then the DA reached in a drawer and pulled out a clipboard.

"I have a list of questions."

"Let's go!" Bobby said.

"Outside of you and Lucky, who else could have known about the murders?"

"Nobody that I know of," Bobby said. "The only person we saw was Javier, the guard at the safe house on the river."

"Who is Javier?"

"Javier is a Cuban man that guards the safe house at night. Carmelo keeps a boat there that we used to go out on and meet the bootleg boat from Lauderdale."

"Did Javier know what you were going to do?"

"No," Bobby said. "All he knew was that we were coming to get the skiff, but he had no idea what we were going to do."

"How do you know that?"

"By the way he acted," Bobby said. "We had been there twice before to get the skiff and he acted no differently. He had no idea where we were going or what we were going to do."

The DA turned back to the list.

"Why do you think Holzafel wanted the judge dead?"

"It wasn't Lucky that wanted them dead," Bobby said. "It was someone else."

"How do you know that?"

"Because I asked Lucky and he wouldn't tell me."

The DA turned back to the list.

"Do you know Mrs. Holzafel?"

"Lucky's wife?"

"Yes."

"I don't know her," Bobby said. "I've heard Lucky talk about her. She lives in Titusville and he lives down here on the boat. I've never met her. Why do you ask me that?"

"Because when you're on the stand under cross examination, Lucky's attorney is going to do everything in his power to make a liar out of you. What kind of army record did you have?"

"Honorable discharge," Bobby said.

"Were there any records that could reflect negatively on your character?"

"Not that I know of," Bobby said.

"How did you meet Lucky?"

Bobby explained his history with Lucky. His work for the big Brazilian when he was a shrimper. Then, after the army on charter trips. When Bobby was finished, the DA sat, quietly pondering the information Bobby had provided.

"Now all of the information about the gambling, moonshining – the bar, the safe house, the trips out to meet the bootleg boat – I want all of that into the record," he said. "You know, I got a sneaking feeling the death of the judge and his wife could be tied to the rackets in this county."

"Maybe," Bobby replied. "Don't be too sure until you have all the information."

Glenn peered at him.

"You know you are one uppity Negro," the DA said.

"Watch yourself," Bobby said. "You promised."

"I know…" the DA said. "Sorry."

The prosecutor returned to his list of questions.

"What about this Carmelo Sanchez?" the DA said. "What do you know about him?"

Over the next over two hours, Bobby answered all of the questions on the DA's list. Finally, once the DA was satisfied, the DA called the deputy.

Once Bobby was shackled again, the DA turned to Bobby.

"Good afternoon, Mr. Lincoln," the DA said, offering his hand.

"Good afternoon to you, sir," Bobby replied. The chains rattled as Bobby shook the DA's hand.

The deputy's face took on a puzzled look as he glanced from one to the other. As he led Bobby out of the office, he shook his head in confusion.

***

The following morning, Bags made his regular visit to Bobby's cell.

"Got some news," Bags said as he stopped the cart in front of Bobby's cell. "The state's going to send me over to Sarasota late next week. They want me to testify in a murder trial."

"How long you be gone?"

"Not sure," Bags said. "According to how long the trial lasts."

"So what you got for me today?"

Bags turned to the cart and handed Bobby two books. One on Hannibal and another on the American Civil War. Bobby took the books and examined them.

"These ought to hold me for a while," he said. "Did you find anything on finance?"

"Not a thing," Bags said. "You plan on being a banker when you get out of here?"

"No, I just want to know about money," Bobby said. "I want to know how money works. I want to know how money makes money. If you can read a book on astronomy and understand how the planets work, couldn't you read a book on finance and learn how money works?"

"Makes sense," Bags said. "Did you know, of all the years I ever had this cart, I never had anybody ask for a book on finance."

"Well, I'm asking," Bobby said, glancing over at the books on the cart. Suddenly, his eyes stopped.

"What's that half a book you got there?"

"That's the front half to Churchill's *The Gathering Storm*."

"Where'd you get it?"

"From the Salvation Army," Bags said. "Lots of books donated to them come to me. Some don't have covers. Some have just one cover. Some have pages missing. I guess I got two or three hundred books in my cell that are in disrepair. Why do you ask?"

"I know where the other half is," Bobby said.

"Come on!!" Bags said.

"No!" Bobby said. "I know where the other half is."

"I was going to throw it away," Bags said.

"Can I have it?"

"Sure," Bags said. "Nobody wants to read just half a book."

"I know somebody that does," Bobby said.

"He must really love to read."

"He does," Bobby replied.

***

The following Sunday, Clifford was back for a visit. First, Bobby asked about his mother, then about Train.

"Train is in jail," Clifford said. "One of the guys at the sugar mill said he had been in there for a while. Something to do about the trouble he got into down south. I went to visit him. He wants to talk to you."

"What about?"

"He wouldn't say," Clifford said. "He said if you would come talk to him, he could blow the lid off the whole shooting match."

"What does that mean?"

"Again, he wouldn't say," Clifford replied. "He wants to talk to you real bad."

"He's in the Blue Springs City Jail?"

"At night," Clifford said. "During the day, he works on the county farm."

***

The following morning, Bobby was back in the DA's office.

"A little bird told me that there is a man at the county farm who can blow the lid off the Chillingsworth murders."

"What?"

"That's what I heard," Bobby said. "I think it would be well worth our time for me to go down and talk to him. He happens to be a friend of mine."

"What is this man's name?"

"Night Train. Night Train Vereen. He's a Jamaican."

The DA got up and went to a file cabinet. After thumbing through several folders, he withdrew a file.

"Would that be Demetrius Night Train Vereen?" the DA asked.

"I never heard Demetrius before," Bobby said. "But I think that's probably him."

The DA handed the file to Bobby.

"Look at this photo," he said. "Is that your friend?"

Bobby examined the photo.

"That's him," Bobby said. "Now if you'll let me go down there and talk to him, we might get a whole new perspective on this thing."

O'Donnell stopped and peered at Bobby.

"What's wrong?" Bobby asked.

"Perspective?" the district attorney asked. "Where did you ever hear a word like that?"

"I read books," Bobby said. "I'm not illiterate."

The DA didn't reply, then returned to the original subject.

"Let me send a county investigator down there to talk to this guy," the DA said. "I can't let anything happen to you."

"Train would never talk to a county detective," Bobby said. "He wouldn't trust him."

The DA peered thoughtfully at Bobby.

"He'll talk to me," Bobby said. "He knows me and he trusts me. This might be the last piece of the puzzle."

"What are you going to ask him?"

"I'm not sure," Bobby said. "He wants to talk to me. He knows a lot about the criminal activity in this county."

"I can't send you down to the farm alone," the DA replied. "Why, if something happened to you, I wouldn't have a case."

"I do know how to take care of myself," Bobby said.

"What if it's a setup?" the DA said. "What if you go down and, when you turn your back, this guy puts a shiv in you."

Bobby laughed.

"I'm a former soldier," Bobby said. "I know how to take care of myself. Moreover, that's not going to happen. I know Train too well."

"Okay," the district attorney said. "Sunday is the best day for this sort of thing. The prisoners don't work on Sunday and this Train will have time to talk to you."

Bobby nodded.

"But remember," the DA said, "you got to be with a guard at all times."

"I know," Bobby said.

"I'll arrange it for next Sunday."

"Big Walter" Huffman

The Wakoola County prison farm was a sprawling one-thousand-acre agricultural operation due west of Wakoola Springs in the deep Glades. On any given day, there would be anywhere from two hundred to five hundred inmates working at the facility raising and canning vegetables, making sugar cane syrup, or cultivating the facility's fifty acres of oranges, grapefruits, and tangerines. Most of the facility's produce was served to prisoners in the county's jails. Some produce, especially citrus fruits and potatoes, were sold to local supermarkets.

The following morning, Bobby, with shackled hands and feet, was in the county sheriff's van going to the county prison farm. It was so good to be outside and feel the wide-open spaces again. Immediately, he thought of Lazarus and wanted to go fishing. Once the sheriff's van was through the front gate, the deputy signed himself and Bobby in, then parked the county car in front of the facility's administration building. Bobby and the deputy went inside and were seated in a detention room. Once Bobby was unchained, he waited for Train.

The moment Train entered the detention room, Bobby drew back in horror. He wasn't wearing his New York Yankee cap, his dreadlocks had been shorn off, and he had severe swelling and bruises on the left side of his face. His left eye had been bandaged over with adhesive tape.

The old friends shook hands and hugged one another.

"Holy Christ!" Bobby said. "What happened to you?"

"Three other prisoners tried to beat me to death," Train said. "If it hadn't been for the guards, they would have done it."

"Oh, man!!" Bobby said. "I'm sorry to see you like this."

"Ain't nothing you can do," Train replied.

"Clifford said you wanted to talk to me."

"Yeah," said Train. "I heard you have turned state's evidence against Lucky. I know you have the ear of the big shots at the courthouse now."

"So what do you want to tell me?" Bobby asked.

"There's an old con that works on the farm who has been involved in the rackets in Lauderdale for years. I been picking tangerines with him the past week."

"What's his name?" Bobby asked.

Train paused as if he feared to reveal what he was about to say.

"Go on," Bobby said.

"Big Walter," Train said. "Big Walter Huffman."

"What does he know?"

"He says he was offered the job to kill Judge Chillingsworth six months before it actually happened."

Bobby took a deep breath, then peered out the administration building window. He knew this was explosive.

"Who offered it?"

"He wouldn't tell me that, but he knows who it was," Train said. "He wants to talk to you directly, but he's expecting something out of it."

"What do you mean?"

"If he provides evidence for a case," Train said, "he's going to want to get something in return."

"Like what?"

"Like getting his term reduced."

"I can't promise something like that."

"That's what he wants."

Bobby peered at Train.

"Why are you doing this?"

"I'm finished with these people," Train said. "They have been owning me and controlling my life for over six years now. I know too much. If I run, they will hunt me down. If they can't find me, they'll kill my mother, then they'll keep hunting for me. I know the way they work. I probably won't get out of this jail alive."

Bobby studied him.

"You know they're coming for you when you get out," Train said. "If you ever get out, they will chase you to the ends of the earth to kill you."

Bobby peered into Train's eyes and slowly shook his head.

"I ain't the running kind," he replied.

"I know you're a big man with your army experience and your judo and all that, but I'm telling you these people will kill you."

He stopped, then took a new tack.

"Remember what I told you last fall?" Train continued. "There is a judge in this county that controls everything. He runs a protection racket for all of the moonshine and *bolitas* operations. Before the cops can raid a place, they have to have a warrant. The police get a warrant from this judge to raid a joint, then he turns right around and calls the joint to warn them the cops are coming. When the cops arrive, there is nothing there."

"Who is this judge?"

"I don't know his name," Train said. "But I've heard the boys down south talking about him. 'Big Walter' will tell you."

"So when can I talk to this Big Walter?"

"Can you talk to the big shots and see if you can get some help with his sentence?"

"I can try," Bobby said. "But I can't make no promises. I'll have to talk to them first. Can I call you here?"

"Yeah," Train said. "Call me. Just leave a message and I'll call back. Tell me if they can do anything and I'll talk to Big Walter."

***

Late that afternoon, Bobby was back in Glenn O'Donnell's office and reported what Train had said. The district attorney was beside himself with excitement at the new revelation.

"What's this guy's name?"

"'Big Walter' Huffman."

Quickly, the district attorney stood up, then went to a nearby filing cabinet and started thumbing through the folders. Finally, he pulled one.

"Walter James Huffman," he said, pulling a file from the cabinet.

Then he reseated himself at his desk, opened the folder, and pulled out a rap sheet.

"Eight years at Raiford for armed robbery. Two counts of assault and battery. Attempted murder. This guy isn't exactly a model citizen."

"In the criminal world, nobody knows more than other criminals."

The district attorney looked at Bobby.

"Yeah," he said. "I know that's true. Okay. Go down there and talk to this 'Big Walter.'"

"Just one hitch," Bobby said. "If he tells you what he knows, he's going to want some help getting his sentence reduced."

"If he helps with this case and provides the information he says he can, I'll write a personal letter to the pardons and parole board in Tallahassee asking for leniency," the DA said. "In fact, I know one of the members of the board. But before I would do something like that, I would expect him to testify to the information under oath."

"I think he will probably do that," Bobby said.

Before leaving the DA's office that afternoon, Bobby called Train at the county farm and made arrangements to meet with him and Big Walter the following Sunday.

***

Big Walter Huffman was a huge black man, every inch of six foot five and close to three hundred pounds. He had big purple lips, a flat nose, jet-black hair with traces of gray, and a constant scowl. Bobby was waiting when he entered the detention room at the county farm.

Bobby shook hands with him.

"Train says you have some information about the Chillingsworth murders," Bobby started.

He nodded.

"Yeah," he replied. "Train said the district attorney could help me with my sentence if I told you what I know."

"That's right," Bobby said. "He said he could make no promises, but he would write a letter to the pardons and parole board on your behalf."

"That's good enough," the big man said. "So what you wanna know?"

"Train said you were offered the job to kill Judge Chillingsworth in the fall of 1954," Bobby said.

"That's right," Big Walter replied.

"Who offered it?"

"Judge Joe Beale," the big man replied. "He's the municipal judge that runs everything in Wakoola County."

"Why did Joe Beale want Judge Chillingsworth dead?"

"He was afraid the judge was going to have him disbarred from practicing law. He said he had to get rid of the judge before the judge got his license."

Bobby was trembling with excitement.

"Do you know anything else about Joe Beale?"

"Judge Joe Beale protects the moonshining and gambling operations in Wakoola County. He protects them by warning them when the cops are coming to raid them."

"Where did you talk to Joe Beale?" Bobby asked.

"There was a meeting between me, 'Bumpy' Robinson, and Judge Beale at a motel in Fort Lauderdale."

"Will you testify to that under oath?"

"Sure will," the man replied.

***

Back in Glenn O'Donnell's office, Bobby reported what Big Walter had said. Upon hearing the information, the district attorney slammed his fist on the table.

"I knew that son-of-bitch was a crook."

He was having an epiphany.

"My God!!" he continued. "Why didn't I think of that? I should have known. Joe Beale had been called before the state bar about a divorce case and the charges were referred to Judge Chillingsworth. I just didn't put two and two together. That's the clincher. Now everything is falling into place."

The district attorney stood up, then peered out the window behind his desk. Then he turned excitedly.

"I always knew it, but I just couldn't put my finger on the truth," he continued. "I never understood how he could drive around in a new Cadillac every year, own homes here and in

Miami, and throw lavish parties for all his friends. Now I know why. He's corrupt!"

He slapped his hands together with pure joy.

***

The following morning, Walter James Huffman was brought to the county courthouse. After a short conversation in which the district attorney promised to write a letter to the Florida Pardons and Parole Board on his behalf, Huffman was deposed. During the proceedings, he testified that Municipal Judge Beale had offered him ten thousand dollars to kill Judge Chillingsworth in November of 1954. Further, he promised to testify to that fact in a court of law.

Once the deposition was complete, Prosecutor O'Donnell called Bobby into his office.

"Now I've got what I need to bring charges against Joe Beale," he said. "Once Lucky's trial is finished, I'll prosecute him. I'll need some time to get an indictment. When the time is right, I'll have him arrested and charged."

"Aren't you afraid this Judge Beale might flee the county?"

"There's no reason for him to run now," he said. "I don't have an indictment yet. Furthermore, he doesn't know that we have talked to this Walter Huffman. We'll come back to Joe Beale. First, I want to get Floyd Holzafel convicted."

***

That afternoon, Bags was back at Bobby's cell to say good-bye. Bobby returned the books on Hannibal and the American Civil War and, for more than an hour, they discussed a broad range of subjects, including history, philosophy, and literature. Most of the conversation was spent on a discussion of Plato's shadows on the cave wall. Near the end, Bobby asked one final question.

"What do you think is the most important knowledge of all?" Bobby asked.

"Self-knowledge," he said. "Plato knew that over two thousand years ago. Nothing is more important than knowing yourself. Study the concepts in psychology and apply them to yourself. You'll discover parts of yourself you never knew were there, but you have to be honest. Without honesty, you will never get to the truth of yourself."

Bobby smiled at the thought.

"The truth of myself," Bobby said, shaking his head with amazement. "What a concept!!"

For a long moment, the two friends peered at one another. Bobby knew Bags was about to say good-bye. He had been dreading this moment.

"Well," Bags said. "I've got to be going. If I don't see you again, I want to wish you good luck!"

"Thanks for everything!" Bobby said, offering his hand.

Bags held Bobby's hand for a long moment.

"You've changed my life," Bobby said. "You have brought out parts of me I didn't even know I had."

"I'm glad I could do something for you," Bags said. "I've always liked to help people. Take care of yourself."

"I will," Bobby said. "You too."

Then, Bobby watched as the old man turned and started pushing the book cart, wheels screeching louder than ever, across the concrete floor to the next cellblock.

Lucky's Trial

Lucky's murder trial was the biggest spectacle to ever be witnessed in Wakoola County when it opened on the morning of April 7, 1956. Curiosity seekers from Miami, Orlando, and Tampa had flooded the sleepy little town overnight. Local hotels and parking lots were full and restaurants had long lines. Reporters came from as far away as New York and Chicago. At the courthouse, hundreds of people packed the corridors and milled about the grounds. At the entrance, young matrons were selling coffee, hot dogs, and sweet cakes, proceeds of which went to the Wakoola County Women's Club. A local printing company was selling little red plastic banners as souvenirs with the words: "Justice for the Judge." A casual observer would have said the atmosphere was one of festive celebration rather than the ominous tones of a murder trial.

By nine a.m., the second-floor courtroom where Lucky was to be tried was packed. The first two rows outside the railing had been reserved for the press. The remaining twelve pews were jammed tight with spectators and both aisles along the outside walls were standing room only. In the balcony, which was reserved for coloreds, a sea of black faces waited patiently for the trial to begin. The courtroom was a dingy affair with high ceilings, brown stains on the walls, and a large clock sponsored by a local funeral home. On the wall behind the bench hung a marble plaque with the inscribed names of the judges who had presided here over the years. Listed sixth was Harold Chillingsworth, 1934-1955. Justice was being sought for the judge in his own courtroom. At one counsel table, defense attorney Carl Richardson, dapper in a white linen suit, was making notes. Across the aisle, prosecutor Glenn O'Donnell waited in front of a stack of court documents, ready to do battle.

A hush fell on the crowd as the court bailiff stepped forward.

"Hear ye, hear ye!!" he said. "The seventh judicial circuit court of Wakoola County, Florida is now in session. Judge Tom Murphy residing. All rise!!"

Behind the bench, the chambers door opened and the judge, a tall, white-haired man in his early fifties, emerged. With a lean, serious face and decked out in his black judicial robe, he had the solemn air of a churchman.

"Gentlemen," he said, rapping the gavel. "Court is now in session."

***

So began Lucky's murder trial. Most of the first day was spent selecting a jury. Once the judge asked Sheriff Cunningham to "call the venire," potential jurors were herded into the courtroom, where each was quizzed about their availability to serve. The group represented a broad diversity of the local populace and they had an endless list of reasons why they couldn't serve. There was a retired mechanic who claimed he was a diabetic. A hardware store owner said he couldn't leave his business. A grapefruit farmer said he was in the middle of spring pruning. An insurance salesman claimed his wife was ill, a commercial fisherman said he didn't believe in the death penalty, and on and on. Among potential jurors, there were no women or Negroes. In Florida, women who wanted to serve as a juror had to file an application with the clerk. Further, most women, being the loving, maternal life-givers, would not relish the thought of sending a man to his death. Negroes, on the other hand, those of sound body and mind, would not want to stand in judgment of a white man.

By lunchtime, the attorneys had whittled the original list of fifty-three potential jurors down to twenty-two. In the afternoon, after much arguing between the attorneys about a potential juror who didn't believe in the death penalty, a jury was finally seated. Twelve white men and two alternates, also white, would sit in judgment of the accused. Now the judge ordered that the defendant be brought into court.

All eyes strained to see Lucky as he was escorted into the courtroom. He looked different. There was no yachtsman's cap and necklace with the gold anchor. Instead of the usual sports shirt and khaki shorts, he was wearing a suit and tie. Clean shaven, his hair had been neatly trimmed and parted in the middle. As he was seated facing the jury, his craggy features exuded a casual, confident smile.

"Mr. O'Donnell, you may begin your case," Judge Murphy said.

State's Attorney O'Donnell stood to address the court.

"Your honor, the state will show that the defendant, Floyd George Holzafel, with malice and forethought, did conspire to kill Judge Harold Chillingsworth on the night of September 29, 1955 by transporting him from his home at Flagler's Point into the Atlantic Ocean, where he was then drowned at sea. The state calls Javier Gomez."

Moments later, a smallish, dark Latino man, maybe thirty-five, was led into the courtroom. He appeared frightened and confused. Once he was sworn in, he took a seat in the witness chair.

"Where were you on the night of September 29, 1955?" the prosecutor asked.

"Working at Indian River Marina," he said with a slight Spanish accent.

"What is your job there?"

"Security guard," he replied.

"Did two men come to the marina that night to get a boat?"

"Yes, sir!"

"Who were those two men?"

"One was Lucky…"

The prosecutor interrupted.

"You mean Floyd George Holzafel?"

"I not know all name, only Lucky."

"Do you see this man in the courtroom?"

"Yes, sir."

"Can you point him out?"

The witness pointed to Lucky.

Immediately, Lucky looked askance at the man.

"Who was the other man?"

"It was a Negro," he said. "Not know name…"

"When they arrived at the marina, what happened?"

"Lucky said they want skiff, then start engine and were gone."

"What time were they at the marina?"

"Close to midnight," he said.

"What were the two men going to do with the boat?"

"Not know," the witness said with a shrug.

"Did you see these two men again that night?"

"Yes, sir."

"What time?"

"Early morning. I guess one or two a.m. They bring boat back."

"Did they say anything about what they had done?"

"No."

"Did you look at the boat after it was returned?"

"Was dark," he said. "Next morning when I leave work, I see blood in boat."

The prosecutor approached the witness and handed him a photo.

"Do you recognize this photo?"

"Yes, sir," the witness replied. "That is boat."

"Your witness."

Defense Attorney Carl Richardson arose from the counsel table and stood in front of the witness. The defense attorney was slender, well tanned, and young, maybe thirty-two or thirty-three, and he carried himself with confidence. In his white linen suit, toothy smile, and well-coiffed blonde hair, he might have stepped off the cover of a fashion magazine. He stood in sharp contrast to the smallish, crudely dressed man before him. In his cultivated southern drawl, he addressed the court in clear, even tones.

"So, Mr. Gomez," he began. "How can you be sure that the man you saw at the marina that night was George Holzafel?"

"I see him before," the witness said, struggling for words.

"Was the moon out?"

The witness shrugged.

"Not remember," he said. "But I know Lucky."

"You mean, Mr. Holzafel, the man who is on trial here?"

He pointed to Lucky.

"Yes, sir."

The defense attorney studied the witness for a moment.

"Mr. Gomez," he said finally, "how many years have you been in the USA?"

"Four," he said, holding up four fingers.

"Do you have naturalization documents?"

"No, sir!"

"Then you are in this country illegally?"

"Yes, sir!"

"How was Mr. Holzafel dressed that night?"

"Was dark," the witness said. "Could not see clothes."

"You could see that the person was Mr. Holzafel, but you couldn't see what he was wearing?"

"I know voice," the witness said.

"What about the Negro? Could you tell the court how he was dressed?"

"No, sir!" he said. "Too dark."

The defense attorney stepped back behind the counsel table and placed his hands on Lucky's shoulders.

"You are telling the court that you are absolutely certain that the person you saw that night was this man?"

"Yes, sir!!"

"You could not have been mistaken?"

"No sir!!"

"Do you understand there at severe penalties for lying in court?"

"Yes, sir!!"

For a long moment, the defense attorney peered at the witness without speaking.

"That's all," he said finally.

Before closing the day's session, Judge Murphy warned the jurors they were not to speak to anyone about the trial except one another. Also, they were to be together at all times and he cautioned them to not read any newspaper articles or watch television shows dealing with the case. The jury foreman assured the judge all of these requirements would be met.

Bobby's Testimony

Although it was late March, the days were miserably hot. The following morning, before court opened, a long line of spectators was queued in the hallway outside the courtroom. As they waited, they read newspapers, drank coffee, and chatted about the case. Women cooled themselves with cardboard fans provided by a local funeral home and men wiped their faces and necks with white handkerchiefs. Once the bailiff unlocked the courtroom doors, the spectators scrambled quickly into their seats.

At nine a.m. sharp, when court convened, the state was ready to present its star witness.

"Your honor, the state calls William Robert Lincoln."

Moments later, Bobby was escorted into the courtroom. He was no longer wearing jail stripes, but a pair of dress pants and a collared shirt without a tie. Prosecutor O'Donnell was well aware he was taking a huge chance in giving Bobby, a Negro, immunity at the expense of a white man. He knew every white man in town was going to be calling him a "nigger-lover," but he didn't have a choice. This was the only possible way for the state to present a case. As Bobby was sworn in, Lucky peered at him like a hungry cat would eye a canary.

"State your name and occupation," said the prosecutor.

"Bobby Lincoln, commercial fisherman."

"Will you explain to the court how you know Floyd George Holzafel?"

Over the next few minutes, Bobby testified that he had known Lucky more than ten years and, during that period, had worked for him in various capacities. At the defense table, Lucky was nervously biting his fingernails.

"When did Mr. Holzafel mention to you that he had a 'big job' he wanted you to help him with?" the prosecutor asked.

"Late September," Bobby replied.

"What did he say this job was?"

"He said he wanted me to drive a boat while he took a man from his home at Flagler's Point out to the Gulf Stream."

"What did he say he was going to do when you reached the Gulf Stream?"

"He said he was going to tie diving weights to the man and throw him overboard."

A hubbub of reactions rippled across the courtroom.

"Order!" the judge said, rapping his gavel.

"So what happened on the night of September 29?"

"Once we got the skiff from the marina," Bobby said, "we took it down the coast to Flagler's Point. Once we arrived at a dock, Lucky said for me to stay with the boat while he went to a house. A few minutes later, I saw lights come on at the house, then I heard voices, then a woman scream."

"Were you surprised when you heard a woman scream?"

"Yes, sir."

"Why?"

"Because Lucky said there would only be one person, a man."

"Please continue."

"A few minutes later, Lucky came back to the boat with a man who had been tied up. He left the man in the boat, then went back to the house. A few minutes later, Lucky came back to the boat, pulling and dragging a woman. After the woman

200

was in the boat, Lucky got in and told me to head to the Gulf Stream."

"Did you know that man was Judge Chillingsworth?"

"No," Bobby said.

"What was he wearing?"

"Faded pink pajamas."

"Please continue."

"So I turned the boat around and headed east. As we headed east, the man kept talking to me."

"What was he saying?"

"He kept saying: 'Listen to me, boy, if you'll take care of us in this, you'll never have to work another day in your life.'"

"He was pleading with you to help him?"

"Yes, sir."

"Please continue."

"After we were halfway out, the engine started overheating and stopped. We drifted for a while. Several times, I tried to start the engine, but it wouldn't start. Finally, the man told Lucky how to fix the problem. Lucky did what the man said and then we were going again."

"What did Mr. Holzafel say after the judge helped fix the engine?"

"He laughed," Bobby said. "He thought it was funny."

Now Lucky was squirming in his chair. He appeared ready to charge the witness and attack him.

"So after Judge Chillingsworth helped get the engine started again, Lucky still wanted to kill him?"

"Yes, sir!" Bobby said. "He laughed. He thought it was funny."

"What was the woman doing during all this?"

"She was kicking and making low sounds. She couldn't talk because she had been gagged."

"What happened when you reached the Gulf Stream?"

"Lucky said 'ladies first,' and he started putting diving weights around the woman's waist. Then, once I saw her face, I recognized her."

"How did you know this woman?"

"My mother had been her housekeeper for a long time."

"That's when you decided you couldn't go on with the murders?"

"Yes, sir. Somehow, she had worked the gag off her mouth and she was yelling at me."

"What was she saying?"

"She wanted to know why I was doing something like this. She asked how I got involved with Lucky and how I could treat her like this."

"What did you do then?"

"I told Lucky I couldn't do it. I told him this woman had been good to me and my mother, and I couldn't do anything to hurt her."

The crowd of spectators leaned forward to hear Bobby's every word.

"Lucky said I was in too deep to get out now," Bobby continued. "He said I was already an accomplice to kidnapping and I was going to prison. Then I told him again I couldn't do it."

"Then what did Mr. Holzafel do?"

"He put his pistol on me and said it was too late to back out now."

"Then what did you say?"

"I thought maybe he was right. So I went ahead and followed his orders."

"Then what happened?"

"The woman was still pleading for her life when Lucky gagged her again with tape. Then we picked her up and lifted her over the side of the boat. As we lifted her over the side, the old man said, 'Remember I love you,' and she made a muffled sound. Then we released her into the water and she sank. When we went back for the man, he jumped overboard. He was swimming away from the boat with the diving belts on him. Lucky said to take the boat to him because we had to kill him. So I started trying to start the engine, but it wouldn't start. It was overheated again. Lucky kept saying, 'He's getting away!! He's getting away!' Finally, I got the engine started and we started searching the water. We couldn't see him."

"He was lost in the darkness?"

"Yes, sir!"

"Then what happened?"

"Finally, we saw him swimming about thirty or forty feet from the boat and Lucky said for me to take the boat to him. When I got close, Lucky started hitting the man in the head with a wood paddle. The man's head was bloody, but he went under water and we couldn't see him again. Finally, we saw him again and I took the boat to him. When I pulled up alongside him, Lucky was trying to hit him in the head with the paddle again, but the man swam away. Lucky was mad now because the man was causing so many problems. Then he reached under the bow of the boat and got a shotgun. While I held the spotlight, Lucky fired the shotgun. There was a lot of blood in the water and then the man sank. Lucky threw the shotgun into the water."

Bobby paused. Although there were more than four hundred people packed into the small courtroom, you could have heard a pin drop.

"Then what happened?"

"We took the boat back to the inlet and left it at the marina."

"The person you call Lucky," the DA said. "Do you see him in the courtroom?"

"Yes, sir!"

"Can you point him out?"

Bobby pointed to Lucky. The big Brazilian was staring daggers at Bobby as their eyes met.

"Your witness!"

The defense attorney stood up to begin his cross-examination, but the judge intervened.

"Gentlemen," the judge said. "The lunch hour is upon us. Court will be recessed until one p.m."

Cross Examination

After lunch, the defense attorney began his cross-examination of Bobby. From the first, spectators could see the dapperly dressed southerner was anxious to attack the witness like a hungry dog would a bone.

"Gentlemen of the jury," he began in his polite southern drawl. "First, let it be noted that the state's witness is a Negro. It is well-known in the south that Negroes are given to lying and cannot be trusted…"

"Objection, your honor," the prosecutor interrupted. "The defense is trying to vilify the witness because of his race."

"Objection sustained," Judge Murphy said.

The defense attorney looked away, took a deep breath, and started again.

"You have been given immunity in this case in exchange for your testimony? Is that correct?"

"Yes, sir!"

He turned to the jury.

"Gentlemen, you are aware that a Negro who participated in the murder of Judge Chillingsworth and his wife is going to go free after this trial?"

"Objection, your honor," the prosecutor said. "The jury is not on trial here."

"Sustained."

Unflustered at the rebuke, Attorney Richardson raked his hand through his hair, then began again.

"Where is your common-law wife Idella?" he asked.

"I think she is with her parents in Manatee."

"In other words, you're not with her?"

Bobby nodded.

"Your honor, could you have the witness answer the question for the record? Head nods can't be recorded into the record."

"Answer either yes or no," the judge instructed.

"I will ask the question again," said the defense attorney. "You are no longer living with your common-law wife? Is that correct?"

"Yes," Bobby said.

"Why not?"

"We had a fight and she went to her parents."

"What was the fight about?"

"She said I hadn't been making enough money," Bobby said.

"Is that all?"

"I got in trouble with the law too."

"You don't really expect the jury to believe that?"

"Objection, your honor," O'Donnell said. "The counsel is trying to badger the witness."

"Sustained."

"I'll ask you for the third time," the defense attorney said. "When your common-law wife left you, what was the argument about?"

"I wasn't making enough money..."

"No! No!" the defense counsel interrupted. "The truth is she left because she learned you were having an affair with Mr. Holzafel's wife? Now isn't that the truth?"

"No!" Bobby replied.

"Is it not also true that you are testifying against Mr. Holzafel so you can get him out of the way? You want him out of the way because you want his wife for yourself."

"No," Bobby said. "That's not right."

The defense attorney abruptly stopped, then turned to the judge.

"Your honor, the defense calls Emilio Sanchez."

"Bring him in," the judge replied.

Bobby stepped down and an early forties, balding Latin man in a flowery shirt was sworn in.

"Name and occupation."

"Emilio Sanchez, electrician."

"Place of residence?"

"Titusville, Florida."

"Do you know the defendant?"

"Yes, sir. He is my neighbor."

"What is your exact address?"

"642 Oleander Avenue, Titusville."

"Where does the defendant live?"

"Across the street at 643 Oleander."

"Mr. Holzafel lives directly across the street?"

"Yes, sir."

"How long have you known the defendant?"

"Ten years."

"Do you know this man?" the defense attorney said, handing him a photo of Bobby.

"Not personally," he said. "I have seen him."

"Under what circumstances?"

"In the late summer of last year, I have seen him going in and out of the Holzafel home late at night."

"Didn't you think that was strange?"

"Yes, sir."

"Why?"

"Because Lucky is married," the man said. "He's not there most of the time."

"What was the purpose of the visits?"

"No idea," the man said. "All I saw was him going in and out of the house late at night."

"Could it have been because Bobby Lincoln was having an adulterous relationship with Mr. Holzafel's wife?"

"It could have been," he said.

"How many times did you see Bobby Lincoln visiting the Holzafel home?"

"Five or six."

"Your witness."

Prosecutor O'Donnell paused before he began his cross-examination. He was very concerned about this accusation. Although he knew it was a lie, he also knew that, if any part of this accusation were proven, it would irreparably harm his case. White men in the South did not take kindly to black men who consorted with white women. He had to disprove every last nuance of this accusation.

"Mr. Sanchez," Glenn started, "how can you be certain that the person you saw going in and out of the Holzafel home was Bobby Lincoln? You said the times you saw him was at night. Mr. Lincoln is a black man."

"I would see him walk under the streetlight that's in front of Lucky's house. I know it was him."

"What kind of car was Bobby Lincoln driving?"

"I didn't see a car," the witness said. "He was always walking when he arrived."

"Mr. Lincoln doesn't own a car," Prosecutor O'Donnell continued. "So how do you think Mr. Lincoln was getting from Palm Harbor to Titusville?"

"I have no idea."

"No further questions," the prosecutor said.

***

When court was recessed for lunch, Glenn O'Donnell immediately left the courtroom and went directly to his office, where he called Tom Morgan, the county's chief investigator. He instructed Morgan, a tall, middle-aged man who wore a white hat and a string tie, to follow witness Emilio Sanchez from the courthouse that afternoon and make a surreptitious photo of him. Once he had the photo, he was instructed to follow the witness to his home. Moments after the first investigator was gone, O'Donnell called in a second investigator and instructed him to go to Titusville and talk to the owner of the home at 642 Oleander Ave.

During the afternoon session, only one witness, a slight, middle-aged white man named Douglas Konopla, took the stand. He was the state polygraph examiner who had conducted Bobby's lie detector tests. After a series of challenges from the defense about his qualifications and his character, he was allowed to testify. Konopla told the court that, regarding his confession, Bobby had answered all of the questions honestly and truthfully.

When Judge Murphy rapped his gavel to end the day's session, Prosecutor O'Donnell was back in his office. The county's photo lab technician had left a photo of Emilio Sanchez on his desk. Once he inspected the photo, he called Bobby into his office.

"Do you know this man?"

Bobby studied the photo.

"I've seen him in Carmelo's, but I don't know who he is," Bobby said.

"Do you know where he lives?"

"No, why do you ask?"

"He claims he has seen you going in and out of Lucky's house late at night. He says you have been having an affair with Lucky's wife."

Bobby laughed.

"I've never even seen her," he said.

"We know that," Glenn said, "but the jury doesn't."

"Train will probably know exactly who he is."

"Can you show this photo to Train?"

"When?"

"Tonight," the DA said. "I need the information fast."

***

An hour later, Bobby was in a county van traveling to the county farm to meet Train again. Once he entered the detention room in the farm's administration building, Train was waiting.

"He's friends with Carmelo," Train said. "His name is Emilio and he owns a club somewhere around Blue Springs. He buys shine from Carmelo."

"Do you know where he lives?"

"No," Train said, "but I would think he lives somewhere around Blue Springs."

"You're sure he doesn't live in Titusville?"

"I've seen his boys unloading shine from the back of a pickup in Blue Springs," Train said. "I don't think his business would be in Wakoola County and his home way up in Titusville."

Surprise Witness

When court reconvened the following morning, the state's first witness was county investigator Tom Morgan. He testified that Emilio Sanchez listed his residence on his driver's license as 102 Sea Gull Lane, Blue Springs, Florida.

"How long has he listed this address as his residence?" Prosecutor O'Donnell asked.

"Six years."

"Now, gentlemen of the jury," the prosecutor said. "How could the defense witness Sanchez have seen Bobby Lincoln going into a home in Titusville when he lives in Blue Springs?"

"That's not unusual," the defense attorney countered. "People put one address on their license, then move and fail to have the address updated on their driver's license."

"It's illegal," Glenn said. "State law requires that drivers maintain their true address on their driver's license."

"All that proves is that Mr. Sanchez failed to put his correct address on his driver's license."

Glenn O'Donnell turned back to the witness.

"Did you follow Mr. Sanchez home after yesterday's day in court?"

"I did."

"And where did he go?"

"102 Sea Gull Lane, Blue Springs."

"And his car was parked there all night?"

"Yes, sir!!"

"Your witness!"

"No questions!"

When the judge recessed for lunch, Prosecutor O'Donnell was back in his office speaking with the county investigator he had sent to Titusville. The investigator said he had not only talked to the owner of the home at 642 Oleander Ave., but he had agreed to come to court that afternoon and testify.

Once the afternoon session started, the state called a new witness.

"Your honor, the state calls Elmer Wallace."

The witness, a graying, slightly hunched-over man who walked very slowly with a cane, was a retired homebuilder.

"You are the owner of the house at 642 Oleander in Titusville?"

"Yes, sir."

"How long have you owned the home?"

"Twelve years," he said. "I built it."

"I understand you rent the property."

"I do."

"Who is the current tenant?"

"Emilio Sanchez."

"When did he rent the property from you?"

"The first of March of this year."

"So, as of today," the prosecutor said, "Mr. Sanchez has only been renting the house for three weeks."

"That's correct."

"So I ask you, Mr. Wallace, if the defense witness Sanchez has only been renting the house for three weeks, how could he have possibly seen Bobby Lincoln going in and out of the home several times last summer?"

"I don't know."

"I know!" the prosecutor said. "Because the testimony of Emilio Sanchez was an outright lie! He said he had been seeing Bobby Lincoln go in and out of the residence at 643 Oleander for almost a year when actually, he had only been renting the home for three weeks. Gentlemen of the jury, it was a lie! A total bald-faced lie!!"

"Your witness!"

"No questions."

When Judge Murphy called for a lunch recess, both Defense Attorney Richardson and his client knew their case was in trouble. The state had absolutely refuted their accusations against Bobby Lincoln. Despite the loss, they had more ammunition.

***

When the afternoon session began, the defense called a new witness. His name was Claude Holzafel, a jowly, early fifties, bald-headed man with a beer belly. He looked very nervous as he was sworn in.

"State your name and occupation," began the defense attorney.

"Claude Holzafel, truck driver."

"Where do you live, Mr. Holzafel?

"Ponte Vedra, Florida," he said.

"Are you a relative of the defendant Floyd Holzafel?"

"I'm his brother."

"Where were you on the night of September 29, 1955?"

"I was with my brother at an Italian restaurant in Jacksonville, having drinks and dinner."

Instantly, a chorus of concerns rippled across the courtroom as spectators strained to hear the witness.

"Order!" the judge said, rapping his gavel.

The defense attorney returned to the witness.

"Do you have evidence which can prove that?"

"Yes, sir, I have a receipt from the restaurant," he said. "I gave it to you."

"Your honor, I would like to enter this receipt into evidence and show this receipt to the jury."

"Objection, your honor," Prosecutor O'Donnell said. "May I see that receipt first?"

"Objection sustained."

Prosecutor O'Donnell stepped across the aisle and took the paper, then returned to his counsel table and started making notes. Once finished, he handed the exhibit back to the defense attorney.

"What I have here is a paid receipt for food at an Italian restaurant named Luigi's in Jacksonville," the defense attorney began, waving the paper in the air. "The bill was for $38.21 and the date was September 29, 1955. It has been marked paid. I submit this into evidence and to the jury for examination."

The defense attorney stepped to the jury box and handed the paper to the foreman who examined it, then passed it along to other jurors.

"Can you tell the court what happened that night?"

"My brother Floyd arrived at my home in the late afternoon. We hadn't seen one another for a while, so we decided to go out for drinks and dinner. We went to Luigi's, one of my favorite restaurants in Jacksonville. We talked, drank some wine, and had a good meal."

"Was there anyone else who saw you and your brother at the restaurant?"

"Oh yes, the restaurant owner, the waitresses, and other people at the restaurant."

"What happened after you and your brother finished your meal?"

"We returned to my house in Ponte Vedra. After we chatted for a while, he said he was tired from the drive and the drinks and asked if he could spend the night. I told him he could spend the night at my home."

"And you were with your brother all night?"

"I was."

"And you said good-bye to him the following morning?"

"I did."

"What time was that?"

"Around 7:30."

Defense Counsel Richardson turned to address the jurors.

"So, gentlemen of the jury," he said in his deep, southern drawl, "if Mr. Holzafel was in Ponte Vedra on the night of September 29 having dinner with his brother, how could he have been somewhere out on the ocean committing a murder as stated by the Negro Bobby Lincoln? This proves, beyond a shadow of a doubt, that Floyd Holzafel could not have committed the murders."

"Your witness."

"No questions, your honor."

"Gentlemen, the noon hour is approaching," Judge Murphy said. "We will recess for lunch and resume at one p.m."

Moments later, Glenn O'Donnell was back in his office with his lead investigator.

"I want you to go up to Ponte Vedra this afternoon and find the manager of this restaurant," O'Donnell said. "Ask him if he knows Claude Holzafel and see if he remembers seeing Lucky and his brother in the restaurant."

***

When the judge rapped his gavel to begin the afternoon session, the prosecutor requested some time for his investigator to complete his work.

"How much time?" the judge asked.

"Can you call a recess until tomorrow morning?"

"Done," the judge said. "Court is adjourned until tomorrow morning at nine."

***

The following morning, before court adjourned, Glenn O'Donnell called Bobby into his office. Once Bobby was seated, the district attorney opened a file folder.

"Remember the young Jamaican?" he began. "The first person you talked to down at the county farm? Wasn't his name Vereen? Demetrius Night Train Vereen?"

"Yeah," Bobby replied. "Why?"

"He was found dead in his cell this morning."

"Oh, no!" Bobby said. "What happened?"

"Somebody put a shiv in him while he was asleep."

"Oh, my God!" Bobby said, dropping his head. "I'm so sorry to hear that. He had been my friend for years."

The district attorney could see tears welling in Bobby's eyes.

"All of his life, he had to fight to survive," Bobby said sadly. "First in Jamaica and then in the States. Fighting to keep his mother and his sister alive. It was like he never had any peace in his life. He was always having to fight to survive."

Bobby inhaled and wiped his tears on the shoulder of his shirt.

"Oh, Train, old friend," Bobby said. "I hope you can rest easy now."

A long pause as the district attorney allowed Bobby to express his grief.

"That's prison life," the district attorney said finally. "Did anybody see you and him talking?"

"Not that I know of..."

"Jails are full of snitches," O'Donnell said. "It's very sad. I'm sorry I'm the one that had to tell you.... Nothing we can do now."

Phantom Witness

Promptly at nine a.m. the following day, Judge Murphy rapped his gavel to begin a new court session.

"Mr. Prosecutor," he said. "Do you have your new witness?"

"I do," the prosecutor replied. "The state calls Luigi Caminetti."

Moments later, a smallish Italian man in his early forties with a neatly trimmed mustache and wearing a flowery shirt took the stand.

"State your name," the prosecutor said.

"Luigi Caminetti."

"Occupation?"

"Owner of Luigi's Italian Restaurant in Jacksonville."

At the defense table, at the moment the witness identified himself, Lucky's eyes grew into the size of saucers. Suddenly, he peered at his attorney in horror as if his doom was at hand.

"There is testimony in this trial," the prosecutor continued, "that on the night of September 29, 1955, the defendant Floyd Holzafel and his brother had dinner at your restaurant. Is that true?"

"No," the man said.

"Why not?"

"My restaurant was closed for repairs from September 20 until October 2."

"Do you know the defendant's brother?"

"Yes, sir," the witness replied.

"He has been a customer at your restaurant in the past?"

"Yes, sir."

"Have you ever seen this man before?" the prosecutor asked, pointing to Lucky.

"No, sir!!"

"Has he ever been a patron in your restaurant?"

"Not that I recall."

"So neither he nor the defendant could have been in your restaurant on the night of September 29, 1955 because it was closed for repairs."

"That's correct."

Prosecutor O'Donnell stepped to the evidence table and took the receipt. Then he handed it to the witness.

"Do you recognize this receipt?"

"No, sir! That's not a receipt from my restaurant," the witness said. "All of the receipts from my business have a Luigi's logo at the top."

"That's an Italian-looking man with a mustache holding a pizza? Isn't that correct?"

"Yes, sir!"

"So what is the origin of this so-called receipt?" the prosecutor asked. "I can tell you the origin. It is a forgery. A forgery designed to mislead and lie to this court."

"Objection, your honor," the defense counsel countered. "There is no evidence to indicate that his receipt is a forgery."

"If the restaurant was closed on the night of murders, how could anyone have written a legitimate receipt?"

The defense attorney peered at the prosecutor for a long moment, then failed to reply.

Prosecutor O'Donnell turned to face the jury.

"Gentlemen of the jury, this is the second outright lie the defense has tried to perpetrate on you and this court. As you can see, they have no case because the defendant is guilty of murder and both he and his attorney know it."

When the judge rapped his gavel to end the third day, all onlookers knew it had been another bad day for the defense. Now Defense Attorney Richardson, the dapper southerner who was smiling and enthusiastic at the beginning of the trial, was sagging at the corners of his mouth. Meanwhile, his client was drumming his fingers nervously on the counsel table.

"Your honor," the defense attorney said, "I don't want to waste the court's time or the jury's time, but I have another witness I want to call."

"Then call him," the judge replied.

"I'm having problems locating him."

"What value can he bring to the case?"

"He also saw Bobby Lincoln at the Holzafel home."

"How long will it take to bring in this witness?"

"I'm not sure," the defense attorney said. "I have an investigator trying to find him."

"Under state law, you have twenty-four hours to produce a witness," Judge Murphy said. "That means by noon tomorrow, your witness will have to be in my courtroom."

"It's a delaying tactic, your honor," Prosecutor O'Donnell said, slamming his fist on the defense table. "He doesn't have another witness any more than the man in the moon."

"I have to follow state law," Judge Murphy replied. "Court is adjourned until noon tomorrow."

***

The following morning, court was reconvened at the judge's appointed hour.

"Where is your new witness?" Judge Murphy asked.

"I'm sorry, your honor," defense counsel said. "I'm still unable to locate him."

The judge slowly shook his head in disbelief, then his face screwed up in anger.

"I have given you the twenty-four hours the law requires to produce a witness," Judge Murphy said. "Are you trying to make a fool of me and this court?"

"No, sir!!"

The judge took a deep breath, bowed his head, and put his hands to his head for a long moment.

"Okay," he said finally. "I'm going to grant you another twenty-four hours to produce this phantom witness. A man's life is at stake here. I would hate to think he was convicted because a witness who could save him was not located. If you have not produced your witness by noon tomorrow, you can rest your case. You are not going to waste the court's time any further."

"It's a delaying tactic, your honor," Glenn said. "The defense is just delaying the inevitable, hoping for a miracle."

"We'll know tomorrow," Judge Murphy said.

Lucky and his attorney looked at one another. From the looks on their faces, it was evident both had been shot in the heart.

Verdict

The following day, promptly at noon, the trial was reconvened for the fifth day. There was still no witness.

"I warned you," the judge said, shaking his finger at defense counsel. "If you didn't present your witness today at noon, this case was going to move forward. Do you have any further witnesses other than this phantom witness?"

"No, your honor," the young attorney said.

"Do you have any further evidence to present to the jury?"

"No, your honor."

"Then rest your case."

"One moment, your honor."

The defense attorney then took a seat at the counsel table and began whispering to his client. Lucky's face screwed up in a frown as he listened. Once his attorney was finished, Lucky was wild-eyed and looked around the courtroom like a ship's captain would look for a port in a storm. Then he responded in angry whispers to his attorney. This brought even more angry words from Attorney Richardson. Finally, Lucky stopped speaking and nodded his head.

The defense attorney then stood up and faced the judge.

"The defense rests, your honor," he said.

"Then the court is ready to hear summations," Judge Murphy said.

Now, five days into the trial, the defense attorney was beginning to look weary. The judge's admonishments, his inability to produce evidence and witnesses, and the unyielding counterattacks from the prosecutor were taking their toll. Young, sincere, and a true southern gentleman, Attorney Richardson had tried to present an honorable defense, but it was looking remarkably thin. He was well aware that he had not created reasonable doubt in the minds of the jurors.

Meanwhile, Lucky himself looked worried. Very worried. The confident smile he had on the first day was gone now. As a fingerprint technician in Oklahoma many years earlier, he had a good understanding of trial proceedings and, at this point, he knew his case was thin. Now he looked nervously about the courtroom, drumming his fingers on the counsel table, his eyes darting about the courtroom in abject fear.

Moments later, State's Attorney O'Donnell stood in front of the jury to begin his summation.

"Gentlemen," he began, standing in front of the jury box. "The state has proven its case beyond a shadow of a doubt. Despite efforts by the defense to lie and mislead you, the state's case has remained solid as a rock in the face of these lies. At every turn, the state has disproven all of the defense's claims. The witness who testified Bobby Lincoln was seen going in and out of the Holzafel home has been proven a liar. Efforts by the defense to make you believe that Floyd Holzafel was at some restaurant in Jacksonville on the night of the murders has also been proven a lie. The receipt the defense presented to support the claim was an outright forgery. I know that. You know that and the defendant knows that. Somebody, somewhere had a blank receipt book from this restaurant. They sat down, wrote a false date and a false food order, then the defense presented it as if it were true. We now know that the receipt is the second of two big lies the defense has tried to get you to believe. Yes, it is true that Bobby Lincoln was given immunity for his testimony, but, under the circumstances, this was the only way the state could legally present its case. With these points in mind, I am asking you to find Floyd Holzafel guilty of first degree murder."

O'Donnell stopped, then turned to face the judge.

"That's all, your honor."

Judge Murphy pursed his lips and addressed the defense attorney.

"Mr. Richardson?"

The defense attorney arose from his seat at the counsel table, then turned to address the jury.

"Gentlemen of the jury," he began in his southern drawl, "I want you to look closely at what is happening in this case. The state's entire case is based on the testimony of one witness, a Negro. A big, black murdering Negro is going free while a white man could lose his life. Is that the Southern way? The way of our forefathers? To put a Negro ahead of a white man in the face of the white man's imminent death? How could you possibly find Mr. Holzafel guilty under these circumstances? How could you sleep at night after rendering a verdict of guilty? Your parents, your forefathers would drop their heads in shame if you find Floyd Holzafel guilty."

He stopped. He was sweating. He withdrew a white linen handkerchief from his hip pocket and wiped his face and neck. His image as a proper southern gentleman was melting almost as fast as his case. At the defense table, Lucky kept staring at his hands, clasped together as if in prayer.

"A courtroom is not only a place where justice is dispensed," he continued. "It is also a cultural tradition where local customs are revered and perpetuated. As white men and as true Southerners, your heritage demands that you find Mr. Holzafel not guilty. If you men call yourselves true southern white men, you will give Mr. Holzafel his freedom. Do you understand? Again, I reiterate. If you convict Mr. Holzafel of murder in this case, you should be ashamed to call yourself white men."

Then, looking tired and exhausted, the defense attorney turned back to the judge.

"I'm finished, your honor," he said.

Judge Murphy turned to the prosecutor.

"Anything else?"

O'Donnell looked first at the judge, then at the jury for a long moment, then he moved to address the jury again.

"Just because the state's star witness is a Negro does not mean he cannot tell the truth. The defense attorney is trying to pervert the intentions of the court by asking you to reach a decision based on personal prejudice. I am asking you to reach a decision based on the evidence which has been presented to you. I am asking you to rely on truth in your decision. Please bear that in mind during your deliberations. Thank you!"

He stepped from in front of the jury box.

"That's all, your honor."

Over the next hour, Judge Murphy charged the jury. He explained the intricacies of state criminal law and noted that if the jury reached one decision, they were to deliver one verdict. On the other hand, if they reached a different decision, they were to pronounce a different, separate verdict. The jury listened intently as the judge dispensed his instructions and, finally, after more than an hour, the instructions were finished.

"Now begin your deliberations," he said.

The crowd of spectators watched as the jury shuffled out of the courtroom to the anteroom. Now they would wait for the jury's decision. Some spectators left their seats to have coffee and sweet cakes while others roamed the corridors and grounds to await the verdict. After two hours of deliberations, the foreman sent a request asking that the jury be allowed to see the restaurant receipt again. The receipt was handed over to the foreman and he returned to the anteroom. Over the next two hours, the court and the crowd waited.

Then, just after 1:30, someone rushed out of the courtroom and shouted into the hallway, "The jury has reached a verdict." Instantly, the crowd of spectators dropped whatever they were doing and rushed back into the courtroom.

Moments later, the jury was back in the courtroom and seated in the jury box. Judge Murphy rapped his gavel.

"Has the jury reached a verdict?"

"We have, your honor," said the foreman.

"Read the verdict."

The jury foreman cleared his throat, then began reading.

"We, the jury, find the defendant Floyd George Holzafel guilty of first degree murder…"

Suddenly, the remainder of the foreman's message was drowned out when loud applause and whoops of pure joy rang out from the colored section in the balcony. Reporters rushed out of the courtroom to call in the news to their editors. A chorus of loud boos erupted from some whites in the main courtroom, while others quietly left.

"Order!! Order!!" Judge Murphy shouted, rapping his gavel.

Once order was restored, Lucky was led from the courtroom in handcuffs. His head was down as he went out, but all could see the contorted, angry rage in his face. It was the end of the line for the big Brazilian.

***

Three hours later, Municipal Judge Joe Beale was arrested in his law office in downtown Wakoola Springs and charged with two counts of capital murder. Two days later, during a preliminary hearing, it was revealed that Judge Beale, fearing Lucky would implicate him in the murders, had tried to have Lucky killed while he was in the county jail. According to testimony, Joe Beale had arranged for a jail trusty to slip a pack of cigarettes to Lucky that contained potassium cyanide. The nineteen-year-old trusty, rather than giving the cigarettes to Lucky, went straight to authorities. This single event brought down the entire house of cards. The moment Lucky learned that Judge Beale had tried to have him killed, he decided to turn state's evidence and testify that Judge Beale had been the person who hired him to kill the judge and his wife. All the parts of the puzzle had now fallen into place.

***

The following day, Bobby gathered all of his personal possessions from his cell. There was a picture of his mother, the half copy of Churchill's *The Gathering Storm*, and shaving gear. Just after ten a.m., a deputy arrived and led Bobby down the stairwell. There were no chains this time. Bobby was a free man. Downstairs, Bobby collected the bag of personal items that had been taken when he was arrested six months earlier. Finally, Bobby was walking down the walkway and into the courthouse. When he entered the DA's office. Glenn O'Donnell was waiting. He was all smiles when Bobby closed the door.

"You've made me a very happy man," he said. "When I took this job, I promised to clean up the corruption in this county. I knew they sold moonshine in these little out of the way honky tonks. I knew they ran women too, but every time I sent a squad of deputies down to raid them, everything was clean. Now I know what the problem was. You've made my promise to the people come true."

Bobby was listening.

"Also, you helped me crack the biggest murder case ever tried in this county," he continued. "If it hadn't been for you, I couldn't have done it."

With that, he stepped from behind his desk and shook Bobby's hand.

"Thanks, Bobby," he said. "Thanks so much."

Bobby nodded his acknowledgement.

"Also," he continued, "I wanted to tell you I've learned some things out of all this. Things about people and race and personal respect. I'm a different person now. I see things differently now. Thanks, Mr. Lincoln!"

Bobby smiled.

"You're quite welcome, Mr. O'Donnell."

Freedom

Twenty minutes later, Bobby and Sheriff Cunningham were riding in a county squad car back to Palm Harbor.

"It's a miracle you got out of his, Bobby," the sheriff said. "An absolute miracle."

"Yeah," Bobby replied. "I guess you could say that."

"Now that it's over, I would leave Palm Harbor if I were you," the sheriff said. "At least for a while."

"Why?"

"Your life could be in danger," the sheriff said.

"Where would I go?" Bobby said. "I can't leave Mama."

"You stepped on the toes of some big operators," the sheriff said. "They aren't going to take kindly to what you did."

"I don't know how to run," Bobby replied. "I'll have to take my chances."

"You're a hard man to get through to," the sheriff said.

"Maybe so," Bobby replied. "But I don't know how to run."

The sheriff didn't reply.

"Where do you want me to take you?"

"To Mama's house," Bobby said.

Twenty minutes later, Bobby said good-bye to the sheriff and got out of the sheriff's car in front of his mother's house. Moments later, as he walked across the front yard, he saw Clifford next door working in the yard.

"Great God!" Clifford called. "Are you a sight for sore eyes!"

Bobby laughed.

"Can you come over and talk to me?"

"Let me see Mama first," Bobby said.

"I'll be waiting," Clifford said.

Bobby's mother was beside herself with joy upon seeing her son again.

"Oh, baby," she said. "I'm so glad to see you. Thank the Lord!! Praise Jesus that my baby is home safe and sound again."

Bobby embraced his mother and they went inside. Twenty minutes later, he was wolfing down a plate of fried chicken, green beans, and mashed potatoes. As he ate, his mother peppered him with a barrage of questions. What was he going to do now? Was he going back to Idella? Could he get his job back at the sugar mill? What was life like in jail? Bobby answered the questions as best he could. For most of the questions, the answer was that he didn't know.

Once Bobby left his mother's house, he went next door to Clifford's. Upon seeing his old friend, Bobby hugged him.

"I can't believe you a free man," Clifford said.

"Well, here I am," Bobby said. "Did you know Train is dead?"

Clifford, a shocked look on his face, peered at Bobby.

"What happened?"

"Somebody put a shiv in him while he was asleep."

Clifford shook his head.

"Those are the same people that's going to come after you," Clifford said. "These people don't mess around. Like I told you, I'd be leaving town if I were you."

"They not going to mess with me," Bobby said.

"You don't listen to nobody. Do you?"

"I guess you could say that," Bobby said.

"Well, I'm happy to see you out of jail," Clifford said. "If you need me, you know where I am."

Thanks," Bobby said, offering his hand.

***

It was just past noon when Bobby arrived home. Inside, there was no electricity. The power had been shut off for non-payment. The food in the small refrigerator had spoiled and was stinking to high heaven. He cleaned out the refrigerator, then, after changing clothes, he headed out the door and started down Coast Trail to Waddell's Grocery. As he walked, his thoughts turned to Idella. For the first time in six months, he missed her. Truly missed her. He wondered where she was and what she was doing. He wondered if she knew he was a free man. At Waddell's, he used the public phone to call her. Her mother answered and said she wasn't available. When he asked further questions, she hung up. After buying bread and some canned goods, Bobby headed back home. He would have to go into Wakoola Springs the next day and pay the electric bill.

Once the food was put away, he wanted to see Lazarus, but he knew the teenager would not be in from school for two more hours.

After retrieving a bottle of shine from the shed, he headed through the palmetto undergrowth to the beach. First, he checked the boat. It had not been touched. Then he continued to the beach. As he slogged through the wet sand, watching the soft foamy waves rush over his feet, his thoughts turned back to the events of the past six months. The soul-searching that led to the confession, his mental expansion from his relationship with Bags and this new way of looking at the world had created a totally new Bobby. It had been a long tortuous journey, but now he had answers to the questions that had dogged him six months earlier.

If there is a God, he told himself, *it is this great sea; forever sleepless, timeless, and endless.* Life, as it existed, did not frighten him. Over the past six months, he had made his peace with the universe as he had found it and he accepted its immutable laws. He knew that energy, and life itself, was neither created nor destroyed; it simply changed forms. When the consciousness of this life had left him, he would remain forever an integral part of this great universe. For Bobby, that knowledge alone was far more glorious than the expectation of a hundred lifetimes. With that knowledge, death had no dominion. Death was a trick, an innate fear against which mankind had constructed many much-needed assurances in the form of organized religion. Knowing that he would always be part of this great universe was all the assurance Bobby needed. This beach was his altar. It was here he found peace and communication with a power infinitely greater than himself. Here he could embrace eternity. Bobby would leave the rapture of the archangels and the trumpets of the Lord to others.

Lazarus

Twenty minutes later, Bobby headed back down the beach to his home. He knew Lazarus would soon be coming home from school. Back at the house, he took a large pot, a loaf of bread, salt, pepper, and a jar of mustard from the kitchen. Then, outside, he grabbed the little engine out of the shed and started to the boat. As he made his way through the palmetto undergrowth, it felt so good to be free, to swing his arms without hitting steel bars or listening to orders from some unfeeling authority. Moments later, he was dragging the boat across the sand to the beach. When he emerged from the undergrowth and arrived at the forest of sea oats, he heard a voice.

"Bobby!"

Bobby peered toward the tarpaper shack. Instantly, he saw Lazarus bounding through the sea oats.

Lazarus ran straight to Bobby and the two old friends hugged one another.

"I'm so glad to see you," Lazarus said. "I missed you!"

"I missed you too," Bobby said.

Lazarus looked inside the boat at the pot.

"What you got there?"

"We going to the blue crab hole," Bobby said. "Then we going to cook and eat crab till the cows come home."

"Let's go!" Lazarus said.

"Look what else I got," Bobby said.

He held out half of a paperback book. Lazarus peered at the object, then at Bobby, not recognizing what he was holding. Lazarus took the object. It was the other half of Churchill's *The Gathering Storm* he had received from Bags.

"Holy moly," Lazarus said. "Wait a minute."

Instantly, he turned and dashed back through the sea oats to the house, Moments later, he returned, carrying the other half of the book. Then taking one half, he matched it perfectly to the other half.

"Well, look at that!" Lazarus exclaimed with pure joy in his eyes. "It's like a miracle."

Moments later, Bobby's boat was skimming north through the blue water past Coronado Inlet. After some ten minutes, they found the secret passage into the cove and, once inside, they gathered more than thirty blue crabs. Then Bobby spun the boat around and returned to the landing at "Sea Oats Cove." There they gathered palmetto fronds to sit on, then built a fire and put the crabs on to boil. The light from the afternoon sun glided their faces in gold as they chatted.

"Whoo-wee!" Lazarus said. "I thought you were gone, Bobby. I mean, gone forever and forever."

"Can't nothing hurt me," Bobby said.

"What's it like being in jail day after day?"

"It's not all that bad," Bobby said. "It's the boredom, most of all; you have to keep your mind occupied. I spent a lot of time reading."

"Were you afraid?" Lazarus asked. "There are some bad people in jails."

"I'm never afraid," Bobby said.

Lazarus looked at Bobby and smiled.

"You've changed since you been gone," Lazarus said.

"How do you mean?"

"Everything about you seems different," Lazarus said. "The way you talk, the way you look, the way you hold your head. All of that is different now."

"How do you know that?"

"I can see it," Lazarus said.

"Yeah," Bobby replied. "I guess you're right. Part of that was because of you."

Lazarus peered curiously at Bobby.

"What did I have to do with it?"

"Remember what you said? 'You don't know how smart you are until you start reading'?"

"Yeah," Lazarus said. "My teacher said that."

"That's what got me started reading in jail," he said.

Lazarus smiled.

"Aw, you don't have to be giving me no credit," Lazarus said. "You're my friend. I'm just glad I could help."

Bobby stood up and checked the pot. The crabs were cooked.

"You ready to eat?"

"You won't believe how hungry I am."

Bobby removed the pot from the fire. Then he poured the boiled crab onto a bed of palmetto fronds.

Lazarus reached for one of the hot crabs, then suddenly dropped it.

"Be careful," Bobby said. "They're still hot."

Lazarus was wringing his hand from the pain.

"Let me get some sea water to cool them off."

Bobby picked up the pot, went to the water's edge, and filled it with cold seawater. Then, one by one, being careful not to get burned, they dumped the crabs into the cool water.

"You're so smart," Lazarus said.

Moments later, the crabs were ready to eat.

They spent the next hour breaking open the crab shells and plucking out the tasty morsels. Once a piece of crabmeat was free of its shell, mustard was applied and it was wolfed down. Finally, they had eaten crab until their bellies could hold no more.

"I always have fun with you, Bobby," Lazarus said. "Always."

"Thanks!" Bobby said.

Fire

By the time they finished eating, darkness had closed in and a misting rain had started. Finally, Bobby doused the fire, said goodbye to Lazarus, and started to drag the boat through the palmetto undergrowth. As he neared the hiding place, he looked up and saw a bright light over the tops of the mangroves. Something was on fire. He wondered what it was. The light was coming from the direction of his house. His house? Quickly, he dropped the rope to the boat and raced through the undergrowth. At the clearing, he stopped and looked on in horror. His house was afire. His clothes, his furniture, his pictures… all of his belongings were going up in flames.

Quickly, he went into the shed, grabbed a bucket, and filled it with water from the rain barrel, then threw it on the fire. It was useless. The flames were too heavily involved. The living room and the kitchen were already destroyed and flames were rapidly moving to the bedroom. He needed to save his clothes. Quickly, he opened a window, then just as quickly, he turned back. The heat and smoke were too intense. Now Bobby knew he was helpless to do anything. For several moments, he stood watching the fire destroy his home.

Suddenly, a shot rang out and Bobby immediately recognized the whizzing sound of a bullet.

Holy Christ, he thought, *somebody is shooting at me.*

Suddenly, Bobby broke into a dead run toward the palmetto grove. As he ran, more shots rang out and he could hear the swishing sounds of the bullets flying over his head. Finally, safely hidden among the palmettoes, he peered out toward the road. In the distance, he could see a black pickup truck with a camper top slowly moving down Sand River Road. Now the rain was coming down harder. Bobby returned to the boat, then pulled it to its hiding place. Moments later, he was lying on the blanket underneath the overturned boat. Above he could hear the heavy raindrops clinking on the bottom of the overturned boat.

He had to think. These were the people that Train and Clifford had warned him about. These were the people who wanted revenge for his testimony against Lucky. Revenge for getting Joe Beale put in jail and being charged with murder. *Who are these people?* he asked himself. Patton always said to know your enemy. What did Bobby know about them? He tried to think. Train had said they just came up on you without warning and started shooting. They had proven that. He tried to remember what else Train had said. If they come looking for you and can't find you, Train had said they go to kill your mother. Suddenly, his heart chilled with fear. His mother was in danger.

Quickly, he shot out from under the boat, raced through the undergrowth, then up Sand River Road.

"Mama! Mama!" he cried as he raced through the driving rain. As he passed Smith's boarding house, he was running faster than he had ever run in his life.

"Mama! Mama!"

Five minutes later, he could see the church and Clifford's house. Then he heard shots. There must have been fifteen or twenty. Then in the distance, through the huge sheets of rain, he could see the same black pickup truck pulling away from the front of his mother's house.

Oh, God! he thought as he neared Clifford's house. *Oh God, I hope nothing has happened to Mama.*

Rain, in great sheets, pelted Bobby as he ran across the yard to his mother's house and bounded up the steps. He feared the worst. As he opened the door, he could see the glass windowpane had been shot out.

"Mama! Mama!" he called.

There was no answer. Bobby dashed through the living room and into his mother's bedroom. His mother was lying in bed.

"Mama!" Bobby said.

His heart fell when he saw his mother. Blood was oozing out of her mouth and running down on the neckline of her white nightgown. Now he could see a bullet hole in the side of her neck.

"Oh, Mama!" he said. "I love you."

Slowly, she turned to face her son.

"I love you too, baby," she said in a whisper. "Sit down and talk to me for a minute."

Bobby took a seat on the bed and took her hand.

"Mama! I've got to get you to a hospital."

"Hospital ain't going to do me no good," she said. "I'm dying. I'm leaving this earth."

"Oh, Mama!" Bobby said, holding her hand in his. "I love you so much! What am I going to do without you?"

Bobby could feel her hand getting cold.

"I don't know, baby," she replied softly.

Slowly, she turned her eyes to face him. Her eyes were deathly pale.

"I can't help you anymore," she said. "The only thing that can help you now is the hand of God."

For a brief moment, she peered directly into Bobby's eyes, then he felt her hand go limp. He knew she was gone. Gently, Bobby folded her hands over her chest, then burst into tears.

***

An hour later, Bobby was at Rev. Jenkins' house across the street. His eyes were swollen from crying. He explained that his mother was dead and asked the reverend if he would take care of funeral arrangements.

"I'll see that your mother's burial is taken care of," he said. "I know she had a little insurance policy that will cover her burial. We talked about that long ago. There will be some papers for you to sign."

"Thanks," Bobby said. "Just let me know what you need."

"When do you want to have the funeral?"

Bobby peered at him.

"Can we do it tomorrow?"

"That's kind of fast," Rev. Jenkins said. "I think I can talk the funeral home into it."

Rev. Jenkins peered at Bobby.

"Is that all?" Rev. Jenkins asked.

"Yes," Bobby said. "There is one more thing. I want you to let me report this to the law."

"You have any idea who would do something like this?"

"I think I know who did it," Bobby said. "That's why I need a few days to gather some evidence before the law knows about it."

"That's fine by me, Bobby," he said. "I'll take care of the funeral and you take care of the law."

"What white people don't know won't hurt 'em any," Bobby said. "At least for a few days."

"Yeah," Rev. Jenkins replied. "News travels kind of slow around here anyway."

"It sure does," Bobby said. "Thanks so much."

Once Bobby was back outside, he walked across the street to Clifford's house. It was dark. He knocked on the door. No answer. Bobby wondered where his old friend was. He needed to talk to him.

***

Over the next day, Bobby remained hidden from sight. That night, he slept under the overturned boat. He knew he couldn't go near his mother's house. They would be waiting. Clifford had bought cornbread, black-eyed peas, and ham for him. That night, Bobby saw the black pickup easing down Sand River Road. He knew they were looking for him. He knew if he appeared on Sand River Road, he could be a dead man because they would shoot him on sight.

An Army .45 and Two Clips

The following afternoon, Bobby, along with Clifford, Lazarus, and other members of the Ebenezer Baptist Church, attended his mother's funeral. It was a graveside service and she was being buried along her husband at the same site where Bobby had cleaned off the grave seven months earlier. Bobby felt safe at the funeral. Surely they wouldn't come for him at a time like this, he felt. Not with so many witnesses and in broad daylight. Then, on second thought, Bobby knew they would probably be watching. He knew he would be watching too.

"And Jesus said, 'let not your heart be troubled,'" Rev. Jenkins said, reading from an open Bible. "You believe in God, believe also in me for in my father's house are many mansions. Were it not so, I would not have told you. And if I go away and prepare a place for you, then I will come again and receive you unto myself that where I am, there ye may be also."

The mourners stood solemnly at the graveside as Rev. Jenkins finished the services. Then, after a short prayer, he motioned for the funeral home personnel to lower the body. As the coffin was slowly lowered into the grave, Bobby peered down Cemetery Road. Suddenly, in the bright sunlight, he saw a glint of metal through the grove of the pine saplings that lined either side of the road. Then, as he peered closer, he saw the dim image of a black vehicle. *That's them,* Bobby thought. *They're waiting for me.*

Quickly, he turned from the services and raced through the tombstones. Once he was out of the graveyard, he sliced through the dense palmetto undergrowth to the point where he had seen the glint of light, then, still hidden by the undergrowth, he cautiously crept to the roadside. Finally, as he neared the road, he got down on his knees and crawled through the undergrowth until he was within thirty feet of the road. Then he stopped and peered through the undergrowth.

There, outside of the black pickup, Bobby saw Pee-Wee and his minions. *Small, medium, and large,* he said to himself. Pee-Wee was leaning on the front of the pickup. The tall one, Jaybird, was sitting on the running board, a shotgun resting between his knees. Dooley was resting on a fender, smoking a cigarette and holding a rifle. All three were peering toward the funeral.

As Bobby studied the three from his hiding place, he smiled with satisfaction. Now he knew who his enemies were. Now he knew what he had to do. He was going to avenge the death of his mother at all costs. Somebody was going to die, he told himself. *It may be me, but I'm going to take somebody with me.* First thing he had to do was get a weapon.

***

As darkness closed in that night, Bobby slipped through the cypress and palmetto undergrowth to the back of Clifford's house. Inside, through the window, he could see his old friend in the kitchen. He rapped lightly on the back door.

Moments later, Clifford opened the back door and stuck his head out.

"Bobby?" he called.

"Yeah," Bobby said, stepping into the light.

Even before Bobby spoke, Clifford knew why Bobby was there.

"They've come for you, haven't they?"

Bobby nodded.

"I told you these guys are professional killers," Clifford said. "They don't mess around."

"Didn't you tell me you had some guns?" Bobby said. "I need an army .45 and two clips."

"Why don't you run, Bobby?"

"It's not a matter of running anymore," Bobby said. "After that they did to Mama, I'm going to kill somebody."

Clifford shook his head.

"I wish you wouldn't do it," Clifford said. "They going to blow you away faster than you can blink."

"I have to do it," Bobby said. "If I ain't got no pride, I ain't got nothing."

Clifford inhaled.

"You really get into some messes," he said.

"I didn't come here to argue," Bobby said. "Can you help me or not?"

Clifford could see he was wasting his breath.

"I got an army .45," Clifford said. "Been shot eight times, but I got only one clip and eight rounds."

"I need two extra clips and about fifty rounds."

"I can't get that until tomorrow."

"What time?"

"Around eight," Clifford said. "After work, I'll have to go over and talk to my friend at Blue Springs. He'll have everything you want."

"How much?"

"For the gun, the clips, and the ammo," Clifford said, "I've got to have one hundred fifty dollars."

Bobby pulled a wad of cash from his pocket and counted out one hundred fifty dollars.

Clifford took the money and looked at it.

"Is this part of the money from…?"

Bobby nodded.

"Okay," Clifford said. "I'll have what you want tomorrow. Meet me here tomorrow night."

***

All of the following day, Bobby remained hidden in the Glades. That night, around eight, he was back at Clifford's house. When he arrived, the house was dark. Bobby waited. Finally, around 8:15, he saw Clifford get out of a cab and start toward the house. He was carrying a bag.

"Cliff!" Bobby called.

Clifford saw Bobby in the shadows.

"Here's the clips and ammo," Clifford said. "Give me just a minute and I'll get the gun."

Bobby opened the bag. Inside were two .45 caliber magazines and a full box of fifty rounds.

Seconds later, Clifford reappeared with the pistol and handed it to Bobby.

Bobby released the safety and checked the action.

"Looks good!" he said. "Just what I wanted. Hadn't had one of these babies in my hand in a long time."

"Anything else?" Clifford asked.

"Yeah," Bobby said.

He put his hand in his pocket and pulled out a roll of bills.

"What are you doing?"

"I'm going to give you this money."

"What?"

"There should be just over two thousand dollars there," he said.

Clifford took the money.

"This is the money from the..."

Bobby nodded.

"You're not going to need this?"

"No," Bobby said, shaking his head. "I hate that money. I don't want any part of it."

"Sounds like you checking out."

"Not yet," Bobby said. "I got a job to do. In case it don't turn out the way I want, I want to have my bases covered."

"So what you want me to do with it?"

"You know Lazarus dreams of being educated one of these days. I want you to take care of this money until Lazarus is ready for college. Then, when he's ready, I want you to see that he gets it."

Clifford inhaled.

"Why are you doing this?"

"Because I hope something good can come out of all this," Bobby said. "I'd like to think I did at least one good thing in this world before I leave it."

Clifford peered at him.

"I'll see that it's done," Clifford said. "I promise."

"I knew I could depend on you," Bobby said. "Thanks!! I gotta go now."

Bobby turned and started back across the yard toward the scrub palmetto.

"Bobby!" Clifford called.

Bobby turned.

Clifford rushed to him.

In the back porch light, Bobby could see he had tears in his eyes.

The two old friends shook hands and hugged one another. Then Bobby turned and started into the scrub palmetto.

"Good luck!!" Clifford said after him.

Settling Up

That night, as he slept under the boat, he dreamed about Idella again. Now that his mother was gone, there was a huge emptiness inside him that longed to be filled again. He dreamed he and Idella were at the movies and she was just laughing and laughing. Then they were in bed making love. He remembered how he loved to thrust his body into hers. He missed her kiss and her touch. He missed the smell of her hair and her breasts. Now he needed her like he had never needed her before.

The next morning, he was up at sunrise. When he awoke, he knew this was going to be one of the most important days of his life. It was a day he very well might die, but he was not afraid. After a meal of cold black-eyed peas and ham, he emerged from the palmetto undergrowth. He knew they wouldn't be looking for him this early, so he went to Waddell's to call Idella. When Idella's mother heard Bobby's voice, she immediately hung up the phone. Angrily, Bobby slammed down the phone.

***

All of that day, Bobby felt like he was in the military again. In the thick cypress and mangrove jungle along the banks of the inlet, Bobby practiced with the army .45. He had forgotten how comfortable an army .45 felt in his hand. This army .45

was a newer model than the ones he trained with in Korea. It had a smoother action, less recoil, and a softer trigger. He preferred the soft trigger. He had bought tin cans for target practice and he remembered and reviewed the ground-fighting tactics he had learned in the army. Now that he had a weapon, he needed a plan. A good plan. *What would Patton do?* he asked himself.

***

That afternoon, Bobby made his way through the palmetto undergrowth behind his destroyed home to "Sea Oats Cove." Once he was in sight of the tarpaper shack, he stopped and waited. He knew Lazarus would be getting in from school any minute. After only five minutes, he saw Lazarus, books in hand, coming through the palmetto foliage. Instantly, Lazarus saw him.

"Bobby!" he called. "What are you doing here?"

"I want to talk to you," Bobby said.

"What you want to talk about?"

For a long moment, Bobby peered at the teenager.

"I want to give you my boat and the motor," he said finally.

"What?" Lazarus said, a shocked look on his face. "You going to give me the boat?"

Bobby nodded.

"Ain't we going fishing no more?"

"Probably not," Bobby replied.

"You going somewhere?"

"Maybe," Bobby said.

"You leaving, ain't you?" Lazarus said, bursting into tears. "Go ahead and say it. You're leaving! I know you're leaving."

Bobby looked at him.

"I guess you could say that," Bobby said.

"Where you going?"

"I'm not sure," Bobby said.

"Will I ever see you again?"

"Yeah, you'll see me again," Bobby replied, his voice breaking. "I'm not sure when, but you'll see me again."

Bobby was trying to hold back the tears. He didn't want Lazarus to see him cry.

"One more thing," Bobby said. "Something else I wanted to give you."

From his pocket, Bobby withdrew the cross his mother had given him.

"I want you to keep this for me," Bobby said. "Someday, I'll see you again and you can give it back to me."

"This is the cross your mother gave you," Lazarus said. "You should keep this."

"No," Bobby said. "I want you to keep it for me. Next time I see you, you can give it back."

Lazarus took the cross. Huge tears were rolling down his cheeks.

"I got to go now," Bobby said.

Suddenly, Lazarus, unable to contain himself any longer, ran to his old friend and threw his arms around him.

"I love you, Bobby," he said.

"I love you too," Bobby said.

Then Lazarus, huge tears rolling down his cheeks, watched as Bobby turned and made his way back into the palmetto undergrowth.

***

Now Bobby needed a plan. He knew they would be looking for him. All he had to do to draw them out was to show himself on Sand River Road near his mother's house. They would come driving slowly along until they saw him, then speed up until they were near, then open fire. First, he considered a running gun battle between himself and the three. In basic training, he had been a master of one-on-one combat and he knew he would have the advantage if it was one-on-one. But, even with his military training, he wasn't sure what the result of three-on-one would be. Moreover, the idea seemed too simple. Too straight forward. He wondered what Patton would do. Tonight was going to be one of the most important nights of his life. It would be a night in which he knew he might live or die. He had to have a plan. A good one.

Bobby knew the thin walls of his mother's house would offer little protection in a gunfight. He needed a stronger, well-fortified position. The concrete walls of the church, he thought, would offer much more protection. He would lure his enemies to his mother's house, then retreat to the more fortified position to actually fight. "Feint, then fight," he told himself. Patton had used the strategy many times during his campaign to retake France. Now Bobby had everything he needed. He had the army .45, two extra clips, a flashlight, and a plan. Now he was ready.

Shootout

When darkness fell that night, Bobby was ready to put his plan into action. First, he slipped out of the palmetto, went to the church, and checked for an open window. The same rear window, the third one from the front on the west side, was still unlocked. Then, he strode across the church parking lot and started walking down Sand River Road. He had a flashlight and waved it in both directions so he could be seen in the darkness. He didn't have to wait long. After only ten minutes, he saw headlights approaching and immediately recognized the black pickup. Then, as the vehicle accelerated toward him, Bobby started running. Once he was in front of his mother's house, he trekked across the yard to the rear of the house.

Seconds later, the pickup ground to a halt in front of the house. All three men got out, weapons drawn.

"All right, nigger," Pee-Wee shouted. "We know you're in there. Come on out or we'll come in and get you!"

Several shots were fired into the house. At the front of the house, Bobby could hear glass breaking and the dull thud of lead slugs burying themselves in wood.

"Jaybird," Pee-Wee said. "Go around to the side. Dooley, take the other side."

Bobby, seeing them closing in, darted into the grove of cypress at the side of the house. More shots were fired into the house. Then, from the cypress trees, Bobby waved the flashlight to reveal his location.

"There he is," Pee-Wee said, pointing into the cypress trees.

More shots were fired.

Instantly, Bobby ducked back into the darkness of the cypress thicket, then made his way out across Sand River Road to the church. The three were now closing in on the cypress grove. Instantly, Bobby flashed the light again to reveal his location.

"He's running!" Pee-Wee shouted. "He's across the road."

Moments later, Bobby shot across the church parking lot and, after opening the unlocked window, he went into the church.

"He's going in the church," Pee-Wee said. "Come on!"

Quickly, Pee-Wee jumped into the pickup while his minions raced across the road to the church parking lot.

Moments later, Pee-Wee pulled the pickup into the parking lot and positioned it so that the headlights were shining through the church windows.

"We got him trapped now," Pee-Wee said, exiting the pickup.

Instantly, he strode to the front of the church and tried the door. It was locked. He shook the door.

"Damn!!" he said.

Then he returned to the pickup.

"Jaybird," he said. "Take this side. Dooley, go around to the other side."

Inside the church, Bobby had taken cover in the center aisle. The wooden pews would provide cover on either side. The headlights of the pickup were streaming through the windows and illuminating the church ceiling. Bobby waited.

Suddenly, on the parking lot side, he saw Jaybird peering through the church window. It was difficult to see inside the church because the white crosses painted on the windows blotted out most of the viewing area. Then, using the barrel of the pistol, Jaybird started breaking the windowpanes and firing indiscriminately into the church.

Blam blam! Blam!

The sound of the shots reverberated between the concrete walls and Bobby could hear the dull thud of the bullets hitting the wooden pews. Suddenly, the shooting stopped and Bobby turned back to the open window. Now he could see Jaybird crawling through the open window. Half-in and half-out of the window, he was an easy target. Bobby took careful aim and fired off two rounds. He heard a moan, then Jaybird fell out of the window and on the ground outside.

Now Bobby turned his attention to the other side. In the darkness, he waited to see which window Dooley would try. Seconds later, he heard glass breaking at the second window, then, crawling along the floor between the pews, stopped and waited for his enemy to make a move. Seconds later, several more windowpanes had been knocked out and shots were fired indiscriminately into the church. Suddenly, Bobby felt an intense pain in his left shoulder. He had been hit. He rubbed his hand over the wound. He could feel the warm blood. Bobby had seen the flashes of yellow light from the gun barrel at the second window. Quickly, on all fours, he made his way to the second window and waited. Outside, in the darkness, he could see the silhouette of Dooley's head trying to peer inside the church. His enemy was less than five feet away. Bobby fired off three rounds in the direction of the silhouette. Then he heard a moan and the shooting stopped.

Now he turned his attention to Pee-Wee. Crawling back along the floor, he made his way back to the window where Jaybird had fallen. He peeked outside. Pee-Wee had Jaybird's arm and was trying to drag him back to the pickup. Quickly, Bobby appeared in the window and opened fire. Pee-Wee released Jaybird's arm, grabbed his leg, and crawled on his hands and knees to the cover of the pickup. Then all was quiet.

***

Moments later, the squeal of a police siren pierced the air and a county squad car with Sheriff Cunningham and a deputy inside pulled into the church parking lot. The sheriff got out and surveyed the scene. Jaybird was lying at the side of the church in front of the broken window. Dooley, after being shot, had staggered back to the front of the church and collapsed. Pee-Wee, who had been shot in the leg, was on his hands and knees, groveling in the gravels of the parking lot.

"Help me!! Help me find my glasses!" Pee-Wee pleaded, frantically feeling around in the dirt. "I can't find my glasses."

The deputy stood over him.

"What happened here?"

"My glasses! My glasses!" Pee-Wee pleaded. "I've got to have my glasses."

Pee-Wee stopped and peered toward the direction of the voice. He was blind without his glasses.

"Who is that?" he asked.

"This is the police!"

"God damn cops!" Pee-Wee said. "I ain't saying nothing till I talk to my lawyer. You understand? Nothing!!"

The sheriff could see Pee-Wee was helpless. He turned his attention to the others.

"Check that one," the sheriff said, indicating Jaybird.

The deputy walked over and peered down at the prostrate form.

"Why, that's Alfredo Gomez," the deputy said. "He escaped the federal prison over in Tampa two years ago."

The deputy bent over and put his ear to the man's chest.

"He won't be escaping anymore," the deputy said.

"What about that one?" the sheriff said, indicating Dooley.

Dooley was lying on his stomach. The backside of his Cuban shirt was soaked with blood. The deputy rolled the body over, then put his ear to his chest.

"This one is gone too," the deputy said.

Suddenly, the church door opened and Bobby stepped out. He was holding his shoulder. Blood was running down his arm.

"Bobby!" the sheriff said.

Instantly, he turned and went to Bobby.

"Are you all right?" the sheriff asked.

"I'm all right," Bobby replied.

"Sit down here and stay quiet," the sheriff said. "An ambulance is on its way."

Bobby, holding his shoulder, took a seat on the church house steps.

"What about this one?" the deputy asked, indicating Pee-Wee.

The sheriff turned, walked back to the parking lot, and stood over Pee-Wee.

"What's your name?" the sheriff asked.

Pee-Wee turned to the sound. He was in a sitting position in the gravel.

"Who is that?" Pee-Wee asked.

"The county sheriff!" he replied.

"Get away from me, you filthy cop," he said. "I ain't saying nothing."

"Come on, get up!" the sheriff said.

Seeing he wasn't going to get any cooperation, the sheriff reached down to pull Pee-Wee to his feet, but the little man shoved him away.

"Get your hands off me, you filthy cop," he said, kicking his feet at the blur in front of him. "I ain't saying nothing till I see my lawyer."

"What do you want to do?" the deputy asked.

"Hogtie him with hand and leg cuffs," the sheriff said.

Instantly, the deputy pushed Pee-wee to the ground, rolled him over on his stomach, and put a knee in his back.

"Turn me loose, you filthy cop," Pee-Wee screamed as the deputy applied the four-way restraints. "Turn me loose. Yaaaaeeeiii!! Get away from me! Yaaaaaeeeiii!! Yaaaaeeeiii!"

Pee-Wee's squeals sounded like a pig being led to slaughter.

Moments later, the deputy had cuffs on Pee-Wee's hands and legs and another securely holding the first two in place. Then, together, the sheriff and the deputy picked up Pee-Wee and threw him bodily in the back of the squad car. All the while, Pee-Wee was squealing like a pig.

As the sheriff slammed the car door, he saw the flashing lights and then heard the siren of the ambulance as it pulled into the church parking lot. The driver got out.

"We got one for the hospital," the sheriff said, indicating Bobby.

The ambulance driver examined Bobby.

"It's a flesh wound," he said, "but you're losing blood. I'll put a tourniquet on it. You'll be okay till we get to the hospital. Come on and go with me."

Bobby, under his own power, started to the ambulance.

The sheriff watched as Bobby and the driver started to the ambulance, then he noticed Clifford standing on the opposite side of the road, watching the proceedings.

"Clifford!" the sheriff called.

Clifford turned to the sheriff.

"Did you see what happened here?" the sheriff asked.

"I sure did," Clifford replied. "These three men came here to kill Bobby."

"I suspected that," the sheriff said. "Can you go into Wakoola Springs tomorrow and make a statement to the district attorney?"

"I sure can," Clifford said.

Suddenly, out of the darkness, a taxicab pulled up in the church parking lot. The door slammed and, seconds later, Idella appeared. For a moment, she frantically surveyed the scene. Then she saw Bobby at the ambulance.

"Bobby!! Bobby!!" she said, rushing over. "Are you okay? I came as soon as I got your message."

"He can't talk now," the driver said. "He's got to get to the hospital."

"Can she go?" Bobby asked.

The driver shook his head.

"Nobody but patients allowed in the ambulance."

"She can go with me," the sheriff said. "I'll provide an escort."

"That's fine!" the driver replied.

"Let's go!!" the sheriff said.

Moments later, as the sheriff's car pulled out of the church parking lot, there was the shattering sound of breaking glass as Pee-Wee's Coke bottle glasses were crushed under the rear wheels.

Reconciliation

Twenty minutes later, Bobby was in the emergency room at the county hospital. Idella had promised to wait while doctors attended to him. After the slug was removed from his upper arm and the wound stitched up, doctors said they wanted him to remain in the hospital overnight for observation. Moments after he was wheeled into a hospital room, Idella appeared at the door.

"Come on in," Bobby said.

Idella, carrying her purse, entered the room and took a seat at Bobby's bedside.

"Thanks for coming," Bobby asked.

"I was worried about you," she said. "Mama said you wanted to talk to me. I heard you got out of the mess you were in."

"Yes," Bobby replied. "I'm a free man now."

"What did you want to talk to me about?"

"I wanted to ask you something."

"What's that?"

"I'm not sure I know how to ask."

"Ask me anyway," she said.

Bobby cleared his throat before he spoke.

"I want you to come back to me," he said.

Idella took a deep breath and looked out the hospital window. For a long moment, she didn't answer, then she turned back to him. Finally, she spoke.

"We can't be together until you are ready to let me into your heart," she said. "We've talked about this a thousand times."

"What would it take to get you to try again?" he asked.

"I'm not sure," she replied. "You're going to have to show more responsibility. You're going to have to show me you really want to be with me and you're committed to me."

"I know I haven't been as devoted to you as I could be," he said. "But I'm not the same person now."

"What's changed?"

"I've been through hell," he said. "I'm a different person now."

She shook her head with indecision.

"Now I'm not going to jump into anything," she said. "I've told you a hundred times I want to be married and have children, but you've never wanted any of that."

"Like I said, I'm a changed man."

She wanted to believe him, but she still wasn't sure.

"Oh, Bobby," she said. "I wish with all my heart that we could be together. I've never quit loving you, but I'm afraid to let you back into my heart."

"Things are different now," he said.

She shook her head.

"You haven't changed, Bobby," she said. "Right now, you'll tell me you've changed so we can get back together, but next week, we'll be right back where we were before."

Bobby shook his head.

"No, that's not true," he said. "Things are different."

Idella peered at him for a long moment.

"No," she said. "I don't believe you."

She paused.

"Why do you want me back?"

"Because I know now that I love you and I need you in my life."

She looked confused.

"Where did all this come from?"

"I told you I've changed."

She peered tenderly at him, then took a seat on the bedside and took his hand. Suddenly, at her touch, a secret part of him, a part that had been buried for almost six months, started to come alive. Her touch was invigorating, cleansing, stimulating. Suddenly, he wanted to hear birds singing, to feel warm sunshine on his cheeks, and the salty mist of the ocean in his nostrils. He wanted to be alive again. He wanted to start caring again.

"So what do you say?" he said, looking into her eyes.

"I'm afraid," she said, kissing him on the forehead. "I'm afraid to open my heart to you again."

She looked away.

"I can't do it again," she said with finality, not looking at him. "My heart can't take anymore."

Suddenly, she stood up from the bedside and took her purse from the chair.

"I'm sorry," she said. "I've got to go now."

She turned and started for the door. As he watched her walk away, Bobby knew this was his last chance at happiness.

"Idella!" he shouted.

She stopped at the door.

Suddenly, Bobby leapt out of the bed and ran to her. Then, several feet before reaching her, he fell on his knees before her. As she watched, he crawled on his knees to her and clasped his arms around her legs. Huge tears were rolling down his cheeks.

"Baby, please don't leave me!!" he said. "Please! Please don't leave me again! I'm begging you."

She heard his pleading tone and peered down at him. She had never heard it before. *Maybe he has changed*, she thought.

She peered at him. She could see the tears.

"Bobby," she said. "You're crying."

"Please come back to me," he said again, wiping the tears with the sleeve of his good arm. "I need you. I need you more than I've ever needed anyone in my life."

Suddenly, she realized that Bobby had changed. His words were sincere. She knew he was speaking from his heart. Unable to contain herself any longer, she knelt on the floor in front of him.

"Oh, baby," she said, pulling his head to hers. "You HAVE changed. You really do need me in your life."

She embraced him, then gently laid her head on his chest.

"So tell me what you want to do," she said, her head resting on his chest.

"I want to go to Manatee and get married," he said. "Then I want to go to Chicago and start over. Didn't you say your sister could put us up for a while till we get on our feet?"

"Oh, yes," Idella said. "She would love to have us. When we get on our feet, could we buy a house we can call our own?"

"If that's what you want," he said.

"I want a little white house with a picket fence and flowers in the yard. Maybe some zinnias and some roses... Could we do that?"

"If that's what you want," he said.

"I'll clean and scrub and mop and dust," she said. "And we'll have a clean house to live in."

She stopped.

"And children," she continued. "Can we have three children?"

"If that's what you want."

"Oh, baby," she said, her eyes filling tears. "You make me so happy!! This is the most wonderful day of my life."

"Then let's do it," he said. "We'll get started tomorrow."

She smiled out of pure joy, then raised her head from his chest, and turned her lips to his.

"Oh, baby," she said. "I love you!"

"I love you too," he replied.

Afterword

The following morning, Bobby and Idella were married in a simple civil ceremony at her mother's house in Manatee. That afternoon, they boarded a bus headed to Des Plaines, Illinois to live with Idella's sister. After only three months, the Lincolns moved out of the sister's house when Bobby found work at a meat packing company. While working days, Bobby attended night school and, in just over three years, he earned a degree in finance. The following week, he began gathering investors for a venture capital firm he had founded and, in less than a year, he had put together enough capital to buy the meat packing company. The following year, he bought two more companies and, four years later, he owned the second largest meat packing company in Chicago. In the year 1963, Bobby was making over one million dollars a month.

***

In 1956, Clifford, using the money Bobby had left with him, bought five acres of land on the west side of the Indian River. Four years later, after a superhighway was built through the property, Clifford sold it for $13,500.00. This was not quite enough to send Lazarus completely through the Negro college in Daytona, but it got him through three and a half years. During his last semester, Lazarus paid for his tuition and board by working in the college cafeteria. In 1966, he graduated with a master's degree in history, then six months later, he took a faculty position at the prestigious Omega College in High Point, North Carolina.

***

Over the next thirty years, Bobby and Idella raised two sons, Clayton and James, both of whom joined the family business. Now at age fifty-five, Bobby decided he wanted to leave something behind for which humanity could remember him. So, in 1985, he spent eleven million dollars to buy twenty acres of prime land in Palm Harbor. Over the next two years, he built a university on the property, which he named Lincoln College for Negroes. It was a very successful college and, during its first year, it had more than 15,000 students. When Bobby learned that Lazarus Jones was a well-respected history professor at a major college in North Carolina, Bobby gave him a call. He asked Lazarus if he would be interested in being the head of his new college. Lazarus said he would make him proud and, two months later, Lazarus was officially named chancellor of the Lincoln College for Negroes. After the induction ceremony, the two old friends had dinner together. Over dinner, Lazarus returned the cross Bobby's mother had given him thirty years earlier.

***

Originally, Lucky Holzafel was sentenced to death in the electric chair for the murders of Judge Chillingsworth and his wife. However, after he testified against Judge Joe Beale, his sentence was commuted to two life terms and the big Brazilian spent thirty-four years in the maximum security prison at Raiford, Florida. During that time, Lucky became a model inmate and joined the prison ministry, claiming that he wanted to help others not make the same mistakes he had. In April of 1990, the Florida Pardons and Parole Board granted Lucky his freedom, noting that he was near death from prostate cancer. Once Lucky was released to his wife, who was still living in Titusville, he died three days later.

***

Joe Beale, the corrupt attorney/politician who started it all, pleaded guilty to two counts of murder and was sentenced to two life terms. Once he was in prison, however, Joe discovered very quickly that prison life was a far cry from the Cadillac and champagne life style he had been accustomed to. Joe found himself eating food he wouldn't feed a dog; he had no privacy and found himself having to defecate in front of other men; he lived in constant fear of other prisoners who would kill for a cigarette. After only three months, Joe had had enough. One morning, when the call officer strode through the cell block, he found Joe's lifeless body hanging from a bed sheet. He was forty-three.

***

After he won the Chillingsworth case, Glenn O'Donnell's name became a household word in the state of Florida. In fact, he became so famous that, the following spring, the Florida Democratic party nominated him as their candidate for the state attorney general's race scheduled for the following November. Glenn handily won the election and, in later years, was elected for three more terms. In 1971, after four terms as the highest-ranking law enforcement officer in the state, Glenn retired to a peaceful life of golf and his grandchildren. He died in 1992 of lupus at the age of seventy-three.

One Thursday morning in March of 1968, Bags Calhoun was waiting on a bench under a palm tree in front of the Wakoola County jail for the bookmobile. When the vehicle arrived, Bags didn't come over immediately, so the driver went to investigate. Bags was dead. He had died while dozing under the palm tree. Nobody ever knew what happened to Bags' body. The same day he died, his body was delivered to the local funeral, placed in a casket, and prepared for burial. Sometime during the night, the body disappeared. When the funeral home director saw the empty casket the next morning, he called the on-duty security guard and asked if anything strange had happened during the night. The guard replied, "Around 2:30 in the morning, I did hear loud singing and the flapping of wings, but I didn't see anybody. It was like something was flying away from this earth to another world."

***

One night in the spring of 2009, Bobby and his oldest son came home from a blues concert they had attended in the Lincoln Park district of Chicago. When he arrived home, Bobby told Idella he didn't feel well and went straight to bed. The next morning when Bobby awoke, he threw his legs over the side of the bed and started to call Idella's name. Seconds later, she was at his side. As she put her arms around his shoulders, he slumped into her breast and, as she held him close, she could feel the breath of life slipping away. "Oh, my dear baby," she cried. "I feel the heat leaving your body. Oh, my dear baby, I know I'm losing you. Oh, God, I know I'm losing you." Moments later, Bobby went limp in her arms. Bobby was dead of a heart attack at age seventy-eight. In his will, he donated more than fifty million dollars to charity and signed over his businesses to his sons. All of his real estate holdings went to Idella, his two sons, and his four grandchildren. As for burial, Bobby requested that he be cremated. In the will, he gave strict instructions that, once his body was cremated and his ashes placed in an urn, they were to be shipped to Palm Harbor, Florida. There, upon arrival, the urn was to be opened and its contents scattered along Sand River Road.

The End

Dear Reader:

Thank you for taking the time to read my novel *The Hand of God.*

If you enjoyed it, please consider telling your friends or posting a short review.

Reviews make a difference.

It only takes a few words and it can help enormously.

Without your reviews and favorable mentions, my hard work might go unnoticed.

Thanks a million for your support.

John Isaac Jones

Editing and formatting by BZHercules.com
Cover art by Patricia Adams from betaimages.com